I0727766

Cross: Three Billy Goats Gruff Retold

DEMELZA CARLTON

A tale in the Romance a Medieval Fairy Tale series

DEDICATION

This one is for Rick and Marcel,
who were kind enough to take me to see
Veluwe and the Delta Works,
Romein's and Julia's dream made real,
even if it took a thousand years..

One

No one should have been abroad with such a storm raging outside, but the man who entered Father's great hall, drenching the flagstones with every step, feared far more than just the storm.

"The sea wall has been swept away. The last of the harvest is lost," he gasped out.

"What of the village?" Father asked.

The man hung his head. "The villagers have already sought high ground, and we will not know how much they have to return to until morning. But with so much water coming through, and the size of the waves…they will need sanctuary for more than a night, while the village is rebuilt."

Father nodded gravely. "On better ground this time, I hope." He clapped his hands. "Summon my men. See to it that every man who can help with the evacuation and rebuilding is on hand, first thing tomorrow morning."

All Romein's brothers rose as one. "Yes, Father." They filed out of the hall, leaving Romein alone at the table.

He got to his feet. "Father, I am almost a man. Please, let me help the relief effort." Younger boys than he served as pages at court, he knew, but Father kept him here at home instead. Likely because the nearest court was ruled over by the Bishop of Maastricht, the mortal enemy of Father, his family and all those who swore allegiance to Father as Count of Gelderland.

Father regarded Romein. "Do you have your sword?"

"It is upstairs, in the chest by my bed," Romein replied. Swords were not worn to dinner, his mother had said so many times he and his brothers knew it was as good as law.

"See that you wear it when you ride out tomorrow. While the others are seeing to the evacuation, you will guard the bridge to Elst. Your job will be to warn anyone who attempts to cross it of the terrible fate that awaits anyone who reaches Elst, or the Bishop's lands at Veluwe."

Romein wet his lips. "What kind of fate?"

"Last time floods swept away the village, many of our people sought shelter in Saint Martin's Church, in Elst. When the Bishop heard, he had them arrested, as thieves and trespassers, and punished accordingly, before I or your grandfather could intervene."

Romein's mouth dropped open in horror. "But it's sacrilege to violate the sanctuary of a church! How could the Bishop get away with it, and not be excommunicated?"

Father shook his head. "The Bishop is the priest's superior, and he denied them sanctuary, seeing as they were already trespassers on his land. They never reached the church. And they cannot be allowed to cross the bridge now, for once they set foot on the Bishop's lands, he may do with them as he pleases. So you must stand firm, and guard the way."

"I will go now, Father," Romein said. Better that he go without sleep than see any of his father's people punished for trying to flee the floodwaters.

"No, you will ride at dawn, and no earlier," Father said. "No one should be out in such a storm."

Romein sank down onto the bench, pushing his plate aside. He had no appetite now. "Yes, Father."

Little did he know that the storm and the flood would be the least of his worries on the morrow.

Two

"The horses have been saddled and packed for an hour or more. Should we not leave?" Julia asked, gazing from William to Thibault and back again.

"We should have been in Elst yesterday, instead of passing the night in some common inn," William said, glaring at Thibault.

Thibault's gaze did not waver from the fighting pit. He flapped a hand vaguely in their direction. "One more round. I have placed a large wager on this bird, and I am certain he shall be victorious."

William seized his arm. "We need to go now, Thibault, before the floodwaters rise any further. If the bridge is washed out, it could be weeks until we reach Veluwe!"

"All the more reason to focus on the cockfight, then, if we are to stay a little longer. The better I know the birds, the more I can win when I bet upon the winner!"

The more he would lose, more like, Julia thought but did not say, for she'd learned quickly that Thibault was quick to anger, and not above cuffing her. Oh, William would chide him and Thibault would shrug it off, saying it was nothing, while Julia was too busy rubbing her jaw or trying to quiet the ringing in her head to argue.

It didn't help that she was dressed like a pageboy, so none of the Count of Gelderland's men would know a prize like the future Lady of Veluwe rode among them, with only two men to guard her. Well, William was a man, though she suspected Thibault was more of a beast. He reminded her of the mean alley cat back home, howling and yowling all night, and attacking any creature that approached him, in between rutting with any female cat he could find.

She'd heard one of the maids calling him the Prince of Cats – the alley cat, not Thibault – for he must be royalty, to lie with so many queens. The other maids had giggled, and a prince the cat had become, though he had but one ear, one eye and no crown.

"William," Julia began.

He hushed her. "You go on ahead, cross the bridge to Elst. Make your way to Saint Martin's Church, and wait for us there. If we have not arrived by dark, tell the priest your true identity, and ask for lodgings for the night. I will make him come."

If only Thibault were not such a large man, much bigger than William by far, she might have believed him. As it was, she knew William would likely have to use the weight of his words to get Thibault to move. And words were something Thibault rarely listened to, unless they came out of his own mouth.

But if she made it to Elst, she wouldn't have to pretend to be a page any more. She wouldn't need to bind her breasts or wear hose that chafed around her hips when she rode. Or fetch food and drink for William and Thibault, like she really was their servant.

"Fine," she said, and marched off. Her palfrey – and it was hers, for the mare did not permit Thibault or William to touch her, let alone sit atop her back – shivered as Julia mounted, as though the horse was just as eager to reach their destination as Julia herself. Julia only had to touch her knees to the mare's flanks and she was off and running.

The inn was soon far behind them, and the river loomed larger. Why, the waters were swirling around the bridge supports, the waves licking hungrily at the bridge itself. She urged her horse to move faster.

Only at the last moment, the palfrey balked at the bridge, prancing about on the river bank as though she'd seen a snake. Julia swore and slid down, wrapping the reins around her hand so that she might walk the frightened creature across the bridge.

Unless the horse was right, and the bridge was more dangerous than staying on the bank…

Julia bit her lip, tasting blood, then sent her magic into the swirling waters, questing, asking. She'd heard that the other elements — fire, earth, air — were not as capricious, and could be commanded. But commanding water was like trying to stop it from flowing through your fingers. You could not force it — only ask.

Today, she asked if the river meant to sweep the bridge away, or if it would hold.

Water never answered in words, but the response was still clear, as the waves calmed, showing her the layers of moss the bridge had collected beneath it over the centuries, proof that it had withstood many floods, and likely would still stand for many more.

Julia inclined her head in thanks, and stepped onto the stones, following the high arch to its peak, before running down the other side, the palfrey's hooves clattering after her.

Until she found her way barred by a naked sword.

"Halt!"

Three

Romein stood guard on the bridge until noon, when the sun vanished behind the clouds. Not a soul had even attempted to cross the bridge. He sighed as he sat down. Father had sent him on a fool's errand again. Well, not precisely a fool's errand, but one where even a fool would be capable of carrying out Father's wishes, without finding himself in the least whiff of danger.

His brothers were likely rescuing people and their belongings from floodwaters, carrying them to safety and beginning to build a new, better village, on higher ground than the first. While he was sitting on an empty bridge, wondering whether the tree that was wedged against the bridge supports would work its way free and continue its journey downstream, or if someone would haul it out of the river to chop into firewood for the winter, when the floodwaters died down.

If he had a pole, like the riverboat men used, he might tip the tree into an angle in the current, so that it could right itself and flow through the bridge and away. Alas, he had no pole, and his sword was too short to reach. A jouster's lance or a spear would do the job. If only Father had given him a spear to carry instead of a sword…

The clatter of a horse's hooves on stone sent him leaping to his feet, drawing his scorned sword. A foot soldier was no match for an armed knight, he knew. He should have remained on his horse, instead of letting her graze in a nearby field while he did guard duty. He should have…

"Halt!" Romein hoped the man running toward him wouldn't hear the tremble in his voice. At least he was leading his horse, instead of riding it.

The man skidded to a stop as the bridge levelled out, and Romein found he wasn't facing a man at all, but a wide-eyed boy, at least half a head shorter than himself. His fine clothes and hacked-off, shoulder length hair marked him as someone's page, for he was surely too young to be a squire yet. Besides, the horse he was leading surely belonged to some great knight, for the mare pawed the ground, eyeing Romein with disdain like a trained warhorse that wanted to trample him into the dust.

Romein lifted his chin. He was more than a match for this page. "You cannot pass. If you wish to cross the bridge to Elst, know that you will pay a terrible toll."

The page frowned. "What sort of toll?"

Romein swallowed. His father had spared him the details, but he knew that the Baron of Maastricht's justice involved frequent use of the lash, and it was rumoured that he was fond of the wheel. The lucky ones were those who were executed after, but he'd heard stories…

"A terrible one," Romein repeated. "The cost will be so great, few survive."

The page looked thoughtful for a moment, then drew his dagger and held it out, hilt-first, to Romein. "I do not have much, but this is the most valuable thing I possess. If I give it to you, will you permit me to pass across the bridge and on to Elst?"

The dagger was beautiful, with waves carved into the hilt, shining silver like the sea in the sun. Whoever this page was, he came from a wealthy family, to own such an ornate eating knife. But a costly dagger would not defend this boy from the Bishop of Maastricht.

"Keep your knife. You have more need of it than I do." Romein waved his sword, before sheathing it. How to explain the Bishop's evil to this boy without frightening him? "There is a monster…"

"Like a troll? My mother told me stories of trolls who guard bridges," the page began eagerly.

Romein found himself nodding. Better that the boy believe in mythical monsters, than men who looked like anyone else, but behaved like monsters. "Yes, just like that. If you cross this bridge, he will take such a terrible toll, it will take more than a lifetime to repay." Romein couldn't suppress a shudder. The worst stories were of men broken on the wheel, crippled for life, forced to labour for the Bishop until he deemed they had repaid him for their crimes.

The page paled. "In that case…thank you, sir, for the warning. My knife will certainly not be enough, but my brothers are coming. They will surely have the means to pay the troll. If you will but let me past, I must reach the priest at the church of Saint Martin before nightfall."

Romein hesitated. If it was up to him, he'd happily let the boy go to church, but the Bishop was another matter. "You'll never reach the church. If the monster knows you have crossed the bridge…"

The page patted his horse's neck. "Epona is swifter than any monster. She will carry me as surely as the wind itself. And no monster would dare set foot in such a holy place as Saint Martin's church, not with the relics of Saint Martin himself beneath the altar. My brothers will see to the monster, you may be sure of it."

Romein shook his head. "You do not understand. No man is a match for the evil Bishop of Maastricht. He is a monster the likes of which would give the devil himself pause."

"Did you hear that, Billy? Not only did that wretched bird lose the fight and all my money, but now we're expected to listen to insults from some troll who looks like he crawled out from under a bridge." Two men on horseback crested the top of the bridge, then dismounted on either side of the page. Almost like they meant to defend the boy against Romein.

"No, he came to warn me about the troll, and the toll for crossing the bridge. A terrible one, by all accounts," the page began, looking from one man to the other. "You must deal with the monster, for is that not why you have come?"

"The only monster I see is some bully telling scary stories to frighten you, and offering mortal insults to his betters," the larger of the two men taunted, stepping up to stand directly before Romein. "What did you say about the Bishop, troll? I dare you to say it again." He seized Romein by the collar and lifted him off his feet.

Romein swallowed. Even if he could draw his sword, the man was too close for him to properly defend himself with it. He should have accepted the page's dagger. "The Bishop of Maastricht is an evil monster, and any man in Gelderland will tell you so!"

The man slammed Romein against the side of the bridge, knocking the wind out of him, then held him out over the roiling waters. "Beg the Bishop's pardon, and I shall let you live."

Romein's arms and legs flailed wildly, looking for purchase, but the man's reach was simply too long. Then he accidentally managed to kick the man in the head.

Fury blazed in the man's eyes for a moment, and then he let go.

Romein screamed as he fell, before he landed hard. Pain exploded and everything went black.

Four

"No, Thibault, don't!" Julia cried, reaching for her cousin.

Her brother William was frozen in horror. No help at all.

They were both too late. Thibault let go, and Julia would remember his terrified eyes and flailing limbs forever, until he hit the tree floating beneath the bridge with an ominous crack and lay still.

"You've killed him!" she screamed at Thibault. "He came to warn us!"

Thibault just shrugged and pushed past her, on his way back to his horse. "You should be thanking me for defending your honour, and your father's," he said, mounting up. "Your father would have had his tongue torn out first for spouting such lies. I did him a mercy." He dug his knees into his gelding's sides, and headed off.

"Come on, we should get going. Thibault wasted enough time. We'll have to spend the night in Elst, before heading on to Veluwe. And pray that there is nothing to gamble on in Elst, or the journey will take even longer." William peered over the side of the bridge and shook his head. "Thibault was right about one thing. Your father never would have tolerated such an insult." He headed for his horse.

Julia could not just leave him lying there. Whoever he was, whatever he'd said…the boy had not deserved to die. She bit her lip, and asked of the water, "Does he live?"

The sound of the boy's heartbeat drifted up to her, magnified by the water.

She dared to breathe again. "Will you please carry him to where he will be safe, and he may receive healing?"

A wave rolled down the river, rebounded off the bank, then lifted one end of the log the boy had landed on. A second wave turned the tree so that it faced downriver, instead of pointing toward the banks. For a moment, it bobbed in the water, before another wave swept it under the bridge, speeding it downstream.

"Protect him," she whispered, biting her lip one last time so the river might taste her magic, and know how much she wanted it to help her.

Another wave crested, carrying the log and its precious cargo around the bend, and out of sight.

Julia peered after it, wanting one last glimpse. Or at least an answer that he would be protected…

"Come on! No wonder this journey takes so long. Just get back on your horse and forget about him. That's what your father would do," Thibault shouted.

Julia sighed. She was not her father, and she would not forget about the boy. He hadn't been wrong — Father's justice was swift and brutal, for she'd seen the evidence of that herself, back home. If the people here had experienced it for themselves, no wonder they said such things about him. But these were her lands now, as they had once been her mother's. Things would be different now she was Lady of Veluwe, she swore.

But she had to get there first. So she slid into Epona's saddle, patting and praising the horse for coming across the bridge, even though it had scared her, and rode into Elst.

Five

Romein woke to an unholy screech, a sound that had chased him through his dreams until he'd fallen and hurt his leg, for it was pain which had awoken him.

"Good, you're awake."

Romein did not agree. He couldn't remember ever hurting so much – his leg felt like it was on fire. "What happened?" For even on the edge of sleep, he knew that a man could not be injured in a dream, only to wake with the same wounds.

"A miracle, I'm certain of it. When I went down to the river to fetch water for the horses, I found you, lying on a log, floating in my millpond. I dragged you ashore, thinking only to give you a suitable burial, but when I touched you, you cried out, for you were not dead. That was this morning, and I've been waiting all day for you to wake. I wanted to send for a physician, but it's only me here, and I have work to do, so I can hardly leave, especially with a sick man in my house…"

"Send for the Count of Gelderland. Tell him to send his physician for me. For…Romein."

"Romein, is it? Well, I am Vermeulen, though most just call me Len. I must finish grinding this batch of wheat, and then I can send the horses out into the field, and set off for Valkhof." Vermeulen nodded. "I shall leave you some supper, and I will return by morning." He left.

The unholy screeching sound resumed. Romein's mind might be fogged by pain, but now he knew the man's name, and that he worked a horse-powered mill, he could repay the man for his kindness. For such screeching should not be borne.

"Tell the Count to bring butter. A whole crock of butter," Romein said. He tried to rise, but pain shot through his leg and blackness swooped in to claim him again.

Six

William insisted on riding into the bailey before Julia, with Thibault grumbling in the rear. On the outside, Veluwe looked like any timber castle, with a sheer ring wall broken only by the open gate, beckoning them to enter. But when she accepted her new home's invitation, Julia could not help but gasp. This was no ordinary castle.

The walls were thicker than she expected, and it wasn't until she stood in the middle of the bailey that she saw why. They weren't just fortifications, but actually parts of the house, enclosed rooms that went right the way around the bailey, until they merged into the main keep, a structure that towered over her.

Julia was vaguely aware of William explaining why they were there to the hastily assembled staff, but she did not want to wait.

"Show me everything," she said to the grey-haired woman, whose hands clutched at the ring of keys tied to her girdle, marking her as the castle chatelaine.

The woman looked startled, then bobbed a quick curtsey. "Yes, milady."

Julia dismounted, and a boy darted forward to take her horse from her. Julia felt a twinge of guilt at not taking care of the mare herself – while pretending to be William's page, she'd had to tend to the horses for much of the journey, a duty she had not minded – but things would be different now. Things would be expected of her, as the Lady of Veluwe.

"What's your name?" she asked the woman.

"Mistress Amma is the housekeeper, Julia," William said. "I'm sure she has other duties. Perhaps one of the maids…"

Father had often said that one must begin as

one meant to continue. Usually, that meant harsh treatment of those who crossed him, but even Julia could see that he was right about making a good first impression – once they'd seen Father's justice, none believed they would ever see mercy from the man.

And Julia was the ruler here, not William. "Mistress Amma, please show me everything," she commanded. "This castle is to be my home now, and I wish to see the extent of my domain."

Amma ducked her head, but not before Julia glimpsed a proud smile. "Yes, milady. The best view is from the top of the keep…" She led the way inside.

Julia puffed a little as she reached the top of the stairs, but the housekeeper showed no signs of distress. She crossed the chamber at the top and flung open the door. "Behold, my lady. The lands of Veluwe."

Julia stepped out onto a balcony that ran right the way around the keep. From here, she could see for miles…why, she'd had no idea the sea was so close!

But from here, she could see far more water

than land, reflecting the clouds as clearly as a mirror. "This is not how my mother described it. She said the lands where she grew up were green, green as far as the eye could see…"

Amma bowed her head. "And so it was when Lady Lia lived here, but the floods have swept away everything. When the waters recede, perhaps the fields will be fertile again. But that is not your concern, my lady, but a matter for the Count. The lands of Veluwe are above the floodwaters, and it is only Gelderland under the water." She leaned over the railing and pointed. "Those are the fields of Veluwe, all harvested and ready for whatever snows the winter might bring. Your flocks are grazing among the stubble, before they return to their usual pastures. Veluwe is the richest part of the lowlands, and the Count of Gelderland surely rues the day your mother refused him, and married your father instead."

Mother must have had her reasons, or perhaps her father had. That was all so long ago.

"But we must hold these lands against the Count, or so my father says. Can we hold?"

Julia asked.

Amma hesitated. "As long as the Count keeps to his borders, and we keep to ours, there has been peace. But should one of his men…or worse, one of ours, trespass…all our men are loyal to your father, milady, and the Count's men, misguided as they are, cleave to him, so when the twain meet, there have been…hostilities…"

"She means fights, cousin," Thibault said, striding out onto the balcony. "One of the village cockfights was between the Count and the Bishop, or at least that's what they called the birds, and it had the largest prize purse of all the bouts put together. Some of the villagers said it was like putting a Bishop's man and a Gelderlander into the ring together — none could predict the outcome, but they would fight to the death for their lord's honour. Of course, they had never seen me fight, or they would know your father's man would win, every time." He flexed his sword arm, making the muscles stand out.

Julia shuddered at the sight of such unsightly bulges. She wished she could order the men not to fight so, but men were hotheaded creatures, driven by their passions far more than reason, and they would fight from when they drew their first breath until they gasped their last, Thibault included.

Thank the heavens Father had chosen to send her here to rule Mother's lands instead of marrying her off to some sword-waving bull of a man with nothing between his ears but an echo of her father's orders.

"Enough talk of men. I wish to see the rest of the castle, Mistress Amma," Julia said.

"And I wish to find the bottom of a wine jug. I think I'll go find the kitchens, or maybe a wine cellar, and leave you women to your housekeeping," Thibault said, disappearing down the steps as quickly as he'd arrived.

"Will your cousin be staying at Veluwe long, my lady?" Amma asked.

Julia shuddered. "God, I hope not. If I have to put up with him another week, I'll push him into the river myself."

Amma made no effort to hide her smile. "Very good, my lady. I have several stout sons who would only be too happy to be of assistance."

Julia couldn't help it. She burst out laughing. She suspected she was really going to like living in Veluwe.

Seven

"His leg is broken."

"Will he ever walk again?"

"Here, drink this, it will numb the pain a little."

"Nothing is certain, but it does not look good."

"What will he do, if he cannot walk?"

"Perhaps the Queen…"

Words washed over Romein, like the waves on the river. Occasionally, just like swimming in the waves, he'd get a mouthful of something foul, but when a voice coaxed him to swallow the bitter brew instead of spitting it out, he did, and the voices dimmed for a time.

Until the voices were replaced by the clattering of wheels on cobblestones.

"Ah, you're awake. The physician said I should keep dosing you all the way to the capital, but he's gone back to Valkhof and it's just us now, so I thought you might want a say in how much of the journey you remember."

Romein blinked, and the blurry face above him became the visage of Benvolio, his cousin. "Did you bring the butter?"

Benvolio laughed. "I did, though the poor miller was mystified as to why. Luckily, you kept asking for it, so I put it into your hands, and even with your eyes closed, you tried to tell me what to do with it. The miller greased his gears and axles and everything else in the mill, for you would not rest until the screeching stopped. Though now we're gone, I have no doubt he'll wash and scrub everything so it's squeaky clean. How he lives with the din, I don't know." Benvolio shook his head. "Now I've answered your question, I have one of my own. How did you come to break your leg?"

Well, that explained the pain. Romein struggled to sit up. With Benvolio's help, he managed it. His leg was encased in a wooden box full of wool, in the middle of a wagon loaded with sacks of the stuff. It did make for a well-cushioned ride. But where…and how…and why? He opened his mouth to ask all this and more, only to see Benvolio's expression. He would receive no more answers until he gave one in return.

Romein closed his eyes. His father had set him one task, and he had failed at it. "A pack of the Bishop's men tried to cross the bridge. I called them to halt, cautioning them against going further. They took insult at this, and set upon me. One of them hurled me over the side of the bridge, into the river below. I thought I had fallen to my death, only to wake when I heard the screeching of the mill. By some miracle, the river carried me into his millpond."

Benvolio looked thoughtful. "Would this lackey of the Bishop's happen to have worn a scarlet cape, as if he thought he was Hugh

Capet himself, swishing it about as he boasted about the score of men he'd beaten on the bridge, until one of my party bit his thumb at him, and the fool was forced to find out the mettle of real Montague men of Gelderland? I broke his nose myself, but between us, we also slashed that pretty cloak to ribbons. I have never seen a man run away so fast!"

Romein cast his memory back. He had not seen the man for but a moment before he set upon him, but now he thought about it... "Yes, the man wore a cloak, but it was faded and dusty, more like rust or old blood than true scarlet. He wore a fleur-de-lis pin, though, made of silver."

Benvolio grinned, and delved about in his pocket for a moment. "Did it look like this?" He held up a silver cloak pin, though the pin itself was bent almost in half.

Romein lay back, satisfied. Whoever the Bishop's man was, Benvolio had most certainly avenged him. "Indeed it did."

"Now, do not tell your father, but I suspect the Bishop's man actually did you a favour, unwittingly and all. While you were missing, a letter arrived from Isaak."

"Who is Isaak?" Romein knew all of his father's men, and he prided himself on remembering their names. He knew of no one called Isaak.

"Our cousin, Isaak. Aunt Maja's son, by Baron Abraham of Rumpelstiltskin. Uncle Chase sent word that Isaak was to serve at court, as the Queen's own ward. You were only a baby then, too young to remember. Actually, you are probably of an age with Isaak. We shall find out when you meet him."

"If he's coming here, why are we in a wagon full of wool?" Romein asked.

Benvolio stared at him. "Why would you think Isaak would come here? He serves the Queen, I said, and he sent a letter. A letter with a note from the Queen herself, offering an apprenticeship for any boy who has an aptitude for all things mechanical with her own artificer." Benvolio coughed. "We have heard rumours that the Queen is collecting scholars at court. Some say she is searching for the secret of eternal life, and only the most skilled alchemists need apply, but others say it is children she wants most, younger sons from noble families, to become apprentices to her scholars and alchemists. Isaak's letter seems to confirm the stories…"

"But why are we going? Am I dying?" Romein prayed it was not so.

Benvolio laughed. "No, the physician says you will live, though he could not say whether or not you shall walk. But if the Queen has collected the finest scholars in the world in her court, looking for the secret to eternal life, then she must also have the best physician. So I convinced your father that he should send you to court, officially to answer Isaak's call for an apprentice, but even if the Queen does not choose you, it is your best chance to walk again." He frowned. "Now, the physician said I am to put a pinch of this powder into a cup of wine, and see that you drink it whenever you wake, so that you will not be in pain for the journey. Or we could not bother with the powder, share the wine, and swap tales all the way to the capital!"

"So your dull tales will put me to sleep, but I shall have nothing for the pain?" Romein teased, though his smile was forced. His leg ached abominably, and every jolt of the wagon only hurt worse. If the physician's magic powder would see that he felt nothing, and slept through the journey, he would welcome its embrace. "I shall moan and groan all the way to the capital, and not have breath to tell you any amusing stories."

"You do not know any amusing stories, for you have not been on any adventures yet," Benvolio said. "Once you've been at court a few months, I wager that will change. Perhaps you will not want come home. Or perhaps you will become the Queen's favourite and the Queen herself, or one of her lovely daughters, will fall in love with you and you will spend the rest of your life at court, and never think of us at Valkhof again." He poured a cup of wine. "So we are to obey the physician, then?" At Romein's nod, he added the pinch of powder, swirling the wine about in the cup until it dissolved. "Drink, and sleep. Perhaps when you wake, we will have already arrived."

Romein drank, and darkness descended. He did not resist it this time.

Eight

For weeks, all Romein saw of court was the four walls of his chamber. Isaak, a boy his own age, was a frequent visitor, and even if he hadn't brought books with him, Romein could not help but like him. They were cousins, after all, and Isaak was full of stories about the wondrous machines he'd worked on with the Queen's artificer, Master Zimmerman.

Looking at diagrams of these machines, either in the books Isaak brought him or drawn by his own hand, was not enough. Romein longed to see them, to understand their workings. So when the Queen's physician fitted his leg with a sort of walking box and gave him a stick to help support his weight, the first place Romein hobbled to was Master Zimmerman's workshop.

He found Isaak in the middle of a small crowd of people, all staring at an enormous wheel that sloshed water from the river into a narrow canal in the city walls.

"By my calculations, the canals should be full within the week, and we should have running water in every town square," a woman said. "Perhaps if we even channelled the rain from the rooftops directly into the canals, opening them up…"

"Nay, if you open the canals, instead of leaving them closed, they will be filled with refuse within a day. They will be open cesspools, and not fit to drink or wash clothes in. Let the rain run to the river as it always has. Or, if you wished to dig cisterns, perhaps…" The man took a piece of charcoal and began to sketch a system of pipes and pits.

Romein leaned forward, fascinated. If an entire city's rainwater could be trained to flow only into such a system, built big enough to hold all the water that came down, the city would never be flooded. If they could build a system of canals back home, forcing the water to flow only where it was wanted, and not allowing it to flood the fields…

"Hey, Isaak, why don't we have such a system back home, so there isn't any flooding?" Romein asked.

Isaak's eyes widened. "I did not expect to see you up and about so soon! And what is this talk of flooding? There's a flood? We must help!"

"The waters have likely gone down since I left, but it floods almost every year back home. It was especially bad this year, for the sea broke down the banks and surged across the fields." Flooding all of Gelderland except Veluwe. The Bishop had surely done some sort of deal with the devil to ensure that his lands were untouched.

"The Queen will know how to help. Could Romein build such canals back home, to stop the flooding?" Isaak asked the woman.

She frowned. "Only if the water has

somewhere to go. It naturally flows to the lowest lying land. If Romein is from the lowlands, then there is nowhere for it to go, and it would take a great amount of work to make it move somewhere else."

"But if we dug deeper in some parts, so they are lower than the rest, surely they could hold some of the water, and drain the surrounding lands," Romein said eagerly. "Not cisterns, but maybe lakes."

The woman pondered for a moment, then said, "Perhaps. You would still need to find a way to make the water move, but as you can see, once you get a waterwheel going, it practically drives itself." She gestured toward the wheel that had occupied everyone's attention only a few moments ago.

A girl perhaps a year or two younger than Romein came running into the square. "Mother, the boys are making Father Tristan tell them all the gory stories in the bible again, and it is time for my lessons. If you do not make them stop, I will miss my lessons again, or I will finish too late to go riding this afternoon. It's not fair!"

The woman frowned. "Your brothers know they only spend the morning with their tutor, and he is yours for the afternoon. You tell them they are to be in Master Zimmerman's workshop the moment they finish their noon meal, and not a second later. I shall be up directly, and if they are still in my bower when I arrive…"

The girl beamed. "Thank you, Mother!" She raced off.

The woman sighed. "Zimmerman, can you examine the new boy while I sort out some domestic matters? If his grasp of water mechanics is as good as it sounds, perhaps he can join Isaak on this project."

Zimmerman bowed. "Of course, Your Majesty."

Romein's jaw dropped, and by the time he'd managed to close his mouth, the Queen had marched off in the direction of the castle. "That was…that was…?"

Isaak grinned. "That was Queen Molina, and her favourite daughter, Princess Rosaline. She means to bring running water to every home in the city, like the legends say the ancients did, but we still have a long way to go yet. The hardest part was bringing the water inside the city. Now that is done… maybe this will actually work."

Water running through every house? The Queen was trying to bring about a miracle. Then again, it would be a miracle if they could stop Gelderland from flooding. Cisterns and pipes and canals and wheels…the cogs began turning in Romein's head, and once they did, they had no intention of stopping.

Thibault stayed for three days. Father allowed William to stay for almost three years, before summoning him home, too.

"I hope she is as lovely a girl as you could wish for, and you love her from the moment you lay eyes on her," Julia said as she bade William farewell.

William made a rude noise. "Father picked her out, so her only virtues are likely her dowry and the influence her family has, and what they can do for Father. It isn't like I need to even bed her – Aran has a wife and several children.

Plenty of heirs to keep Father happy. But it is not me you should be worried about. Once I am married, his eye will fall upon you again, and he'll pick a husband for you next, so you have children you can pass Veluwe onto. I shall do my best to convince him to give you someone nice, for I don't imagine there are many men who deserve you. Few women could manage lands as well as you do Veluwe."

William only thought that because he had not seen Veluwe before the floods. Only half the fields had yielded a decent harvest this year, with the rest still full of salt. And the salt encroached more every year, turning fertile fields into desert.

"I do what I can," Julia said. Lately, that meant supplementing their stores with fish caught from the little sailing boat she ventured out in every morning. William did not know about that, either.

She waved to him from the gate, then ascended the tower and watched him until he was too far away to see. It would be four years more before another member of her family arrived in Veluwe and sought to interfere in her life, but after seven years as the Lady of Veluwe, she knew her people as well as they knew her, and they would stand firm to hold the land they fought the sea for, every day of their lives. Gone was the girl who'd dressed as a page for her journey here, and, while some days she might long for the silks she'd worn in her father's house, most days she preferred her woollen gowns, which could withstand the salt that blew in off the North Sea.

As it was now, for she could see another storm brewing. She clattered down the steps, calling for Amma to make sure everything was secured before the arrival of the coming storm.

Ten

"Good morrow, cousin."

Romein recognised Isaak's cheerful voice, but he did not let up. Parry, thrust, and parry again…if he was a better swordsman, perhaps she would reconsider, look upon him kindly, instead of…

"How goes your suit with Rosaline?"

Romein growled, and overreached. Mercutio stumbled back to avoid Romein's sword and landed flat on his back, with a sword at his throat.

Until a blade crossed his, and he was forced

to contend with Isaak instead.

"I asked you how you fared with Rosaline," Isaak repeated.

"Out of her favour, where I am in love," Romein said, lunging at Isaak.

Isaak was the better fighter, and he had not Romein's lame leg to contend with, so he danced back, sword at the ready, with a grin still on his face. "Alas, that love, which I had thought so gentle, should be so tyrannous and rough in proof!"

"He would not be so rough with Princess Rosaline!" Mercutio said, clambering to his feet. He winced, for several of Romein's blows would likely bruise on the morrow.

"But Princess Rosaline will not have him, for she has her heart set on a political marriage, where she will be a queen like her mother. One such as she will never marry some country lord, whose first love is waterwheels, with which he means to save his country!" Isaak's grin never wavered. "You should forget her, cousin, and go home as you planned. You have learned much from the Queen and from Master Zimmerman. You must now take your knowledge home, and use it to save your people from the floods, as the Queen intended. Meanwhile, Rosaline will likely be married off to some old man who needs heirs, and when she is done labouring for him, she will hear tidings of your triumph, and regret the poor choice she made today. Because you, the hero of your people, will have your choice of ladies falling at your feet."

Romein dropped his guard, holding his free hand up in surrender. "I might save my people from the floods, but if you think I can love another as deeply as I have loved Rosaline, you are mistaken. She is one woman my heart can never forget."

Isaak sheathed his sword. "Ah, but we are both about to set out on impossible quests. You mean to save your people, a far harder task than winning one woman's heart, if it belonged to anyone but flint-hearted Rosaline, and I am supposed to find and save the Queen's eldest daughter, before my family's curse claims me, as it has all my predecessors. Yet you do not waver. I believe you truly will save your people, and I...the Queen is certain that I will save her daughter, though we both know I am no match for the formidable witch who stole her as a baby." He shook his head. "You speak of impossible quests, and yet…"

Romein sighed. Isaak's story was a pitiful one, with little chance of happiness before its end. "Forgive me, cousin. You are right, of course. The Queen has given me a task that may take a lifetime, but at least I know I shall have that. If you carry your father's curse, you will die young, like all the Rumpelstiltskin men. I pray that you may have your miracle, and that you shall find this girl, who your father believed could break the curse, so that you may live a long and happy life at your family estates, which the Queen will return to you after you find her lost princess. Perhaps one day I shall look forward to a visit from you, so that you can show your new bride my miraculous waterwheels, for surely the princess cannot help but fall in love with the man who saves her from the witch…"

Isaak's smile was sad now. "If that is so, then we will both have our miracles. I will introduce my bride to yours, as you show me the lands you have saved. Do we have an accord?"

Romein shook Isaak's hand, not wanting to let go, for he knew this might be the last time he saw his cousin. The Rumpelstiltskin curse had claimed every man in his line but him, and he had precious little time left before it would take him, too.

"Farewell, and may God go with you. For without Rosaline, I travel alone," Romein said.

"But not, I think, for long," Isaak said.

Romein could only shake his head. He could walk the world thrice over, and never find Rosaline's equal. But let Isaak believe what airy fantasies he would, for he had a far darker path to tread.

Eleven

Perhaps William had taken her luck with him. Or perhaps Veluwe was cursed. The salt waters which had left Veluwe untouched for so long were now claiming the land for her own. Four years of increasingly poor harvests, losing field after field to salt. There was not even enough fodder for the dairy cows. If Julia did not go out fishing every day, she might have no meat at all for her table.

She did not keep a fine table, not like her Father did, but even she had seen the stores in the cellar dwindle, never quite replaced by the next year's harvest.

Men who had worked the fields at Veluwe all their lives, like their fathers and grandfathers before them, melted away, likely to seek work with the Count of Gelderland, and Julia could not blame them. They had families to feed, and she had little to spare.

It wasn't until she headed to the orchard to oversee the apple harvest that she saw just how bad things had become. Instead of apples, the trees sported a coat of salt crystals, turning the leaves to brown parchment and the branches to sticks only suitable for kindling. She wanted to weep, for the fertile lands lost, but she knew her people looked to her, so instead she stood strong and ordered the dairy herd reduced to salt beef, for she could see no other way to survive the winter.

Today, standing atop the tower, she could see nothing but desolation. There was no sign of the rolling green fields her mother had loved. The only things rolling now were storm clouds, mirroring the waves below, as the first winter storm brought what could only be a new spate of flooding to her already ravaged lands.

A sob caught in Julia's throat. She had failed. Failed her people, failed her land, failed her mother. Now, her only hope was to head home to her father's house, and beg for his help to restore her mother's lands. For without a miracle, she was about to lose Veluwe to the sea.

She allowed herself time only to pack her things, before saddling Epona and heading back across the bridge.

Twelve

Romein kicked the waterwheel and swore. There was nothing wrong with it. He'd constructed it just like the ones he'd made in Zimmerman's workshop, and connected it to the mill exactly as the designs said he should. Yet the wheel scarcely moved, and if the wheel did not move, then it could not draw water from the flooded field into the channel like he wanted it to do.

It could not be the wheel. It must be the river, which lacked the great snowmelt fuelled currents in the river that ran beside the capital.

The Maas was scarcely a river at all, for it was as lazy as a lake. There was water aplenty, but no power in it which he could harness. Now, if he could harness the ever-present wind, that might work…

A small, one-man sailboat plied the waters, far off into the distance. Its sails harnessed the wind well enough. If he could only attach sails to the wheel, and make it turn…

Romein ducked inside the mill for some paper and charcoal, and began to draw.

Thirteen

A sound somewhere between a screech and a creak began to sound in Julia's ears. It was like no bird she'd ever heard before, but a bird it must be, or a whole flock of them, for no door could keep creaking for so long.

Epona flicked her ears irritably. She heard the sound, too, and she did not approve of it. It took all of Julia's stubbornness to make her keep moving forward, for Epona evidently wanted to turn around and head back to Veluwe as much as her mistress did.

The sound grew louder, the closer they got

to the bridge. But it wasn't until they reached the top of the stone arch that Julia saw it was no bird at all.

A giant wheel, like something that belonged on a cart the size of a house, sat beside the riverbank, turning slowly in the current. What made the wheel more remarkable still were the enormous sails sticking out the side of the structure – and the whole thing creaked in protest as it turned.

The storm was fast approaching, bringing with it strong winds that filled the sails, making the contraption groan even louder…until one of the sails suddenly snapped off, and took flight.

Epona whinnied in fright as the sail headed straight for them on the bridge, and bolted.

Julia, too distracted by the curious sight, was a moment too slow reaching for the horse's reins, so that when the horse moved, she found herself flying backward, toward the edge of the bridge and the river below.

She bit her lip, sending out a desperate plea to the water to protect her, before she landed on the river's surface, which felt as hard as any rock. Her breath blew out as pain exploded in her chest, and she wasn't even sure if her cry for help left her lips before blackness claimed her.

Fourteen

The page blurred before him, and Romein let his mind wander into a daydream. In it, the north wind deposited a sailboat at his door, begging him to board, before sending the boat soaring up into the air, blowing it all the way back to the capital, where he could see crowds forming to celebrate a wedding. Princess Rosaline stood before the cathedral, in a gown tossed by the wind, but there was no sign of her husband. For a moment, Romein dared to hope, and his boat skimmed across the stones in the square, before being whipped up, higher than the highest tower, as the wind changed, sending his boat tumbling back the way it had come, and he helpless to stop it. The stars in the sky hung low, peering at him as though to mock him for daring to look so high, until he feared for his life, for if he was to drift on the high air currents for the rest of his days, then he should surely die, and die alone.

His heart filled with lead, he offered up a prayer to God or fate or whatever other power in the universe had steerage of his course, that it would direct his sail true.

But the answer he received was not the one he wanted.

Romein heard the ominous crack and he raced outside, just in time to see a sail break off and flap toward the river. He swore. This was his second attempt at making a sail wheel, and it was an even bigger failure than the first. The Queen and Zimmerman would know what he'd done wrong and how to fix it…but he had no idea where to start. There must be some better way to make the sails and fasten them to the wheel so they did not snap off and go sailing away on their own.

He sighed and sat down to write a letter to the Queen. He told them everything he had tried, even drawing diagrams of his failed sail wheels, then sealed the letter and asked one of the men toiling away in the salt works to take it to the capital and put it into the hands of Master Zimmerman.

He only hoped he would receive an answer soon, and a better one than fate had offered him.

Meanwhile, he'd best try to retrieve the sail that had taken flight, to see if he could fasten it back on the waterwheel.

Romein set off along the riverbank, dodging the reeds as he searched for his lost sail. He walked for more than a mile before he decided the stupid thing must have sunk, and headed home.

Only to find the sail had made its way into the millpond instead, just as he had on the day Vermeulen found him. Only Vermeulen was gone now, and Romein was responsible for the mill, which also meant fishing out debris from the millpond. He reached out with his billhook, catching the spar the sail was wound around, and dragged it toward shore.

It wasn't until he tried to lift the sail out of the water that he realised it had gained some cargo during its journey – a woman's body. She must have drowned recently, for she hardly looked dead at all. An angel, fallen to earth.

A dove consigned to the crows, called too soon. Beauty too rich for use, for earth too dear. Had his heart ever known love before this moment? He swore it could not, for he had never seen true beauty until now. He dared not profane this angel with his rude hand, and yet, he longed to touch…just her hand, perhaps…

Then she coughed, and groaned. Startled out of his reverie, Romein waded into the pond to save her. The chilly water set his teeth chattering, so he could scarcely imagine how cold she must be. He carried her inside to the warmest place he had, his box bed, then built up the fire, hoping to have a pot of soup ready for when she woke.

He hung her things before the fire, so that they might dry, for he had no other women's clothes for her to wear when she awoke. Her gown was made of fine, heavy wool – like Queen Molina might have worn while working outside. Whoever this woman was, she was no commoner.

But it was her girdle that interested him most – for sheathed at her waist, she'd carried a curiously ornate eating knife. He'd seen such silver waves before, but it took him some time to remember when. The last time he'd seen a knife like this one, it had been in the hands of a boy who rode with two of the Bishop's men – men who had thrown him into the river, and turned him into a cripple.

Surely there could not be two such knives. If this was the same blade, though, that meant this woman was…what? The boy's wife? For the boy was likely a man now. One of the Bishop's men…

A man who would come looking for her, for they could not have been wed long. And what little he'd seen of her as he bundled her out of her clothes and into his bed, he knew had been fair indeed.

Romein sighed. He'd be wise to send her on her way the moment she awoke, or better yet, as soon as her clothes dried. If the Bishop's men knew the Count of Gelderland's son had undressed one of their wives and put her into his bed…Romein would have a fight on his hands, and he knew the Bishop's men did not fight fair. No, they would make sure they outnumbered him, and no amount of sparring with Isaak over the last seven years would prepare him for the beating they'd give him.

As if to remind him, rain began drumming on the roof above. The first of the winter storms was here.

He closed his eyes. Beating or no, he could not send a woman out into the storm. The Bishop's men might be cruel enough to do so, but his own father had raised him better than that.

A broken sail, a waterwheel that wouldn't work, and a woman who belonged to the enemy asleep in his bed. And a storm raging outside, that would likely do so for some days yet. Romein wasn't sure whether to laugh or cry at such a run of bad luck.

So he settled down in the chair by the fire, to wait for whatever his abominable luck would bring next.

Until a distressed whinny from outside reminded him that the mill ponies were not yet in the stable for the night, and he headed out to take care of them, too.

Fifteen

The sound of rain woke Julia, for it sounded much louder than the patter of raindrops on the thatched roof of the keep. This was an incessant drumming that seemed to echo through the room, if a room it was. A place so dark must surely be a cellar.

But not one of Veluwe's cellars, for she knew those intimately. She reached out, and her fingers grazed wood almost instantly. The ceiling wasn't far above her head, either, as though someone had stuffed her into a large chest and closed the lid. At least they'd given her blankets and a mattress, though it seemed they'd taken her clothes in exchange.

She tried to raise the lid, but no matter how hard she pushed, it did not seem to want to budge. Swearing, she set her back against the wall and tried pushing with her legs instead.

Only, it wasn't the roof that moved, but the wall behind her, pitching her out onto a cold floor. She snatched up the nearest blanket and wrapped it around her before anyone could see her nakedness, only to discover she was alone in a circular room, and what she'd taken for a chest was actually a box bed, which took up most of the room.

But there was a chest, and it contained an assortment of men's clothing. Better than nothing, she decided, as she found a tunic and hose that fit well enough. It was almost like pretending to be a page again, as she had on the journey to Veluwe, though those clothes no longer fit her. She'd given them to one of Amma's grandsons.

Dressed, she ventured down the stairs. On the level below, a fire burned in the hearth, while her clothing was draped across the table and benches. Hmm, almost dry. She must have slept for a while if someone had had the time to wash and dry her gown and her underthings.

The smell of something delicious drew her back to the fire. Ah, there was a soup pot on the hearth, keeping warm. It was a rich, meaty stew, judging by the smell, so whoever lived here was not poor.

They probably ate better than she had these last few months, for all that she was the Lady of Veluwe. She sighed. Stealing their dinner was beneath her, though she couldn't deny she was tempted. She had coin to pay for it in her saddlebags, but those were on Epona's back and she…

Now Julia remembered. Epona taking fright at the flying sail, bucking her off, and she'd landed in the river. Well, that explained why she'd been naked – her clothes had likely been soaked. That still didn't explain the searing pain in her side that made it hard to breathe, though.

Another glance around the circular room, bigger than the bedchamber above, gave her the clue she needed to orient herself. This was the mill she'd seen beside the wheel in the water. So the miller had likely been the one to pull her from the river. That explained the rich stew, too, for most millers were not poor — she'd paid enough for flour these last three years to know that. She would have to thank the miller's wife for washing her clothes while she slept.

A door slammed somewhere, and the sound of heavy footsteps tromped up the stairs. The man dropped his heavy bags on the floor beside the fire, then stared at her for a long moment, before he exclaimed, "The boy from the bridge!"

Julia blinked. The boy from the bridge? She hadn't thought about him for years. And yet, now that she looked at this man, it had to be… "You!"

Sixteen

There was a fine horse in the field among the ponies, prancing about with saddlebags strapped to her back. A familiar horse, though he could not remember where he'd seen it before. This was the lady's horse, which had likely thrown her, Romein decided. Perhaps he'd seen her out riding in Valkhof. Well, the lady was not going anywhere tonight, and her horse would need shelter as much as the mill ponies, so he led the way into the stable, gave them their feed, and closed the door.

Only when the mare had her nose deep in

the feed trough did he dare approach to remove the lady's bags. The horse eyed him warily, as though she was considering trampling him to death for daring to approach her, before deciding that the apple in the trough was far more worthy of her attention.

Romein threw the bags over his shoulder and headed back to the mill. He hung his wet cloak up just inside the door, so that it wouldn't drip anywhere else, and headed upstairs to check on the woman.

Only to find her awake and in his kitchen, wearing a set of Vermeulen's clothes. Romein's breath caught in his throat. Instead of an angel, now she looked like a boy. Then there was the knife, and that horse…

"You're the boy from the bridge," he blurted out, then bit his tongue. She was not a boy at all, but on that day, he'd thought she was.

She stared at him a moment, before recognition kindled in her eyes. "You!" Then she ducked her head, shaking it sorrowfully. "I feared you'd died. That Thibault had killed you, and I had not been able to stop him."

So Thibault was the oaf's name, was it? "I fear neither of us were a match for him that day," Romein said.

"I am sorry. And now, you have saved me, when I could not save you?"

He shrugged. "I did not do much saving. You washed up in my millpond, on a raft of sorts. A sail that had come off my waterwheel. I was looking for the sail, and I found you. I brought you inside…oh, and your horse is in the stable, with the mill ponies. I brought your things." He gestured at the bags lying beside his feet.

"I thank you."

He expected her to grab the bags and go upstairs to change into more appropriate clothing, but she just stood there, perfectly comfortable in the dead miller's tunic. By all that was holy, he could see her legs! Sure, they were covered in hose, but the woollen hose clung to every curve, showing just how shapely they were. He'd tried not to look as he undressed her, but now he could not seem to tear his eyes away from her.

"I can pay you for your hospitality. And a

hot meal, if you have enough to share."

By God, he'd forgotten about the soup. Thank all the saints he'd at least taken it off the fire so it wasn't burned to ashes now.

"More than enough for us both, and a fresh loaf of bread, too. The baker in the village, one of his sons is employed in my salt works, and he is kind enough to bring fresh bread every morning. My family see to it that I never run out of butter…" It was a standing joke among them that when he'd been rescued by the miller all those years ago, he'd asked for butter, and Benvolio never let him forget it. The mill never screeched like it had for Vermeulen, either, though, so he was glad of it.

Her eyebrows shot up. "Butter? Oh, it has been too long since we had butter at Veluwe. When we lost the best pastures to salt…" Then she pressed her lips together and shook her head, as though she'd said too much.

So she was in some way beholden to the Bishop. He'd heard stories from some of the salt workers, who claimed to have left Veluwe, but that didn't sound like the Bishop's usual tactics. He insisted on loyalty until death – the

Bishop would never allow even the lowliest of his servants to leave him and take up with the Count of Gelderland. "So it is true, then, that the jewel of the lowlands does not sparkle as brightly as it once did?" Romein asked carefully.

She hung her head. "I only wish I knew why. The floods are all I can think of, but the water never touched Veluwe, yet the salt crept up into the fields like some malicious imp had sown it there in place of seeds. I fear I may have to desert Veluwe entirely. Only a few trusted servants remain."

If she weren't a woman, Romein would have suspected he was speaking to the Bishop himself. Unless she was the Bishop's wife…the men had said a lady ruled at Veluwe, but the Bishop would never let a woman rule in his stead. Why, even his own father would not trust a woman to rule. And while Queen Molina was capable enough, she was still only Queen Consort to her husband, King Lubos.

"And what does your husband say about it?" Romein asked.

The girl burst out laughing. "Oh, I have no

husband, nor am I likely to ever find one, if we lose Veluwe."

Relief rushed through him. She wasn't the Bishop's wife, then. Good.

"Shall we eat? I have a bottle of mead I'd been meaning to save until Yule, but tonight seems a good enough night to share it. It will go well with the stew, and chase off any chill you took from your dip in the river. I could bring up some butter, too."

"I would be most grateful," she said.

Things were fetched, the table was set, mead was poured…and for the first time in his life, Romein found himself sharing a meal with an enemy. She might look like an angel, but if his suspicions proved true, she might be the devil's own spawn. Worse, when he glimpsed her pretty smile, beneath those laughing eyes, he feared he did not dislike it as much as he should. In fact, he did not dislike her at all.

Seventeen

By the time they'd finished their meal, the rain had slowed to a drizzle, which the miller declared was fine enough weather to return to fixing his waterwheel.

Julia sighed. The miller was a very pleasant sort of man, and she wanted to know more about his waterwheel and salt works, and why he'd given the wheel sails, but she knew she couldn't stay. She needed to ride home to Father, to tell him about the sorry state Veluwe had fallen into, and ask for his help to fix it.

She rose, smoothing down the sides of her

tunic. That was another thing she owed the miller – for reminding her how she ought to travel.

"I thank you for your kind hospitality, and for the loan of these clothes. I'd be happy to pay you for them, as I do not know when I will come this way again, and I truly must be off."

He stared at her for a long moment. "It is not often I am blessed to have such a charming dinner companion. Please, take the clothes as a gift, and your company is payment enough. I wish you well on your journey, though I admit I am curious."

"Yes?" she prompted.

"Why do you travel as a man? When you first arrived here seven years ago, and again now?"

As a man himself, the miller had likely never had to consider such things before.

"It is not safe for a woman to travel alone. There are men who might do her harm." If the Count of Gelderland caught wind that the Bishop of Maastricht's only daughter was travelling alone on the road, he would send men to capture her for sure, before forcing her to relinquish Veluwe to him. Father had said so enough times. "My father felt it safer for me to travel in disguise then, and I doubt the world has changed so much that it is any safer now. Especially as I do not have the travel companions I did then." Not that Thibault had been much protection. The number of times they'd gotten into trouble because of him.

But if William were here…

"You must miss your brothers," the miller said, as if reading her mind.

She did miss them. Both William and Aran had been protective, as older brothers always were, but their protectiveness had always been founded in their love for her. But both were likely married now, with children of their own to protect. If she wanted a protector, she'd have to hire one. Or find a husband, which was probably what her father would expect. Her father probably already had some poor sod picked out, waiting to woo her, as soon as he could spare the man to send him to Veluwe. So Julia would be doing her father and her future husband a favour, then, in coming home.

She shivered. She should wear her cloak as she rode, to keep the cold and the rain off her. The rest of her now dry clothes, she shoved into her saddlebags with her other possessions. Then she headed outside to find her horse.

Epona allowed Julia to lead her out of the stable amiably enough, and stood still to be saddled. Julia would miss being able to do things for herself, as she had for so long out here. At home, Father would expect her to let the servants do the work, while she stood by and looked useless. Worse, she'd feel useless, too, for there would be nothing for her to do but sewing and embroidery. If Father found out how well she could sail, or how swiftly she could gut a fish, he'd probably expire in horror.

Funny, she'd rather catch and gut a thousand fish, and sail straight through a storm, than head home to Father right now to confess her failure. But duty called her, and Julia had always been a dutiful daughter.

She set one booted foot in the stirrup, and swung up onto Epona's back. Or at least she tried to. Pain lanced her side, stealing her breath and threatening to steal her sight, too.

Strong arms caught her, easing her down onto the ground again as Julia struggled to breathe. Just inhaling left her sobbing.

"Easy, easy. You must have broken your ribs. You can't ride with broken ribs. You must stay here and rest until they are healed."

She couldn't stay. She had to go to Father. To tell him…

"What would you know? You're a miller, not a physician. Why, you can't even make sails properly," she snapped, though her voice was not as strong as she wished it to be. "Your sail broke off and spooked my horse, or she would not have thrown me. Any injuries she has done me, I can surely lay the fault for them at your feet."

He chuckled softly. "Ah, but I've fallen and broken my ribs, too, thanks to the ministrations of your brother. I know exactly what that feels like."

Oh, by all that was holy…her pain now was penance for not stopping Thibault all those years ago. "Cousin. Thibault is not my brother, he's my cousin, and a bastard cousin, at that."

"Ah, I could have told you he was a bastard on the day I met him. But it's funny. I know your cousin's name, for you have mentioned it before, but I do not yet know yours." He rose, then bowed in such a practiced fashion, Julia swore he must have spent time at court. "I am Romein, the current owner of this establishment, which I hope to greatly improve."

Yes. With sails and strange wheels. Julia would not have believed it, if she had not seen his contraptions with her own eyes. She sighed. What did it matter if the miller knew her name? It was likely a common enough name for girls in these parts, for it had been her mother's and her mother's before her. "I'm Julia."

He took her hand in his and kissed it. "I am honoured to have met you, Julia, and I look forward to listening to many a lecture from you on my shortcomings in sailmaking, until you are fit to continue your journey."

Stay…here? With him? Julia blinked. Well, if she could not sit upon a horse, nor ride home to Father, of course it followed that she could not head back to Veluwe.

"Thank you." While the words fell from her lips unbidden, she was grateful. For deep in her heart, she did not want to leave.

Eighteen

She stood and watched while he climbed atop the waterwheel and took down the sails, working in haste to finish the job before the lull in the storm passed and the wind picked up.

Julia could not do much to help, except pluck the sails from the river when he dropped them, snagging them with his billhook before pulling them to shore.

"The river current was not enough to push the wheel, so I thought if I used the wind as well, it might help. There was a small sailboat in the distance, and so I thought of using sails," Romein explained, letting another sail fall into the water.

She waded in up to her knees and hooked it, dragging the sail out of the river. She wondered if it was her sailboat he'd seen, for most fisherman took their boats to sea, where they might net a finer catch than a few river fish. She had only her own supper to catch, while they had whole families to feed.

"But as you say, I must be doing something wrong. I have never seen a sailboat torn asunder like these were." Romein frowned at the last sail, before tucking it under his arm to wade ashore.

"That is because few fishermen are foolish enough to take their sailboats out in a gale, and if they do, they reef their sails, not run before the wind. A sail must move, to catch the wind as it changes…" Julia shook her head. It had been seven years since she'd learned to sail, and she did most things by instinct now, for the old fisherman who'd taught her had not been a man of many words. She could not talk the miller into being a fisherman, any more than her words could wish a new sail into existence.

Romein reached her side, then turned to regard the water wheel. "So what you're saying is that I must look more closely at a sailing boat, and rig the sails to the wheel accordingly…"

"No! If you want a wheel to turn in the wind, then you make a wheel that catches the wind, like the one the ponies turn in the mill yard, and then somehow make that turn the other wheel that you want…" Oh, this was even worse. Now she was trying to teach milling to a miller, for heaven's sake, when she scarcely understood how one wheel could move another, even when she watched them in action.

Romein's mouth dropped open. "Oh my God, you truly are an angel. A saint sent from heaven itself. Of course. We use sails, but we also use wheels and cogs, axles and gears. Then get those to turn the waterwheel and…" He seized her shoulders and kissed her.

Julia's heart stopped. An eternity passed, though it was but a moment, before he released her, and she dared to breathe again.

"Forgive me, dear angel, for such a passionate kiss of peace, but I was overcome with gratitude. Tonight, I shall attempt to draw what your divine inspiration has made appear in my head, and you shall tell me if it will sink or sail."

She might be able to breathe, but her voice had not yet returned, so Julia only nodded as Romein gathered up the sails to take them inside, where they would be safe from the storm. But the storm brewing within her breast, sparked by that kiss, would prove far more dangerous.

Nineteen

Julia wasn't sure how she ended up sewing the sails for Romein's new wind wheel, or whatever it was he was calling it today, but it kept her busy inside the mill while Romein banged away in a corner of the stable, fastening together the spokes of the wheel, the spars that would hold the sails.

She reasoned that she could sew as well, if not better than any man, and though she would not call herself a sailmaker, nor had she ever made her own sails, the sails had never come off her boat, so she had to be better at sailmaking than Romein.

The sound of hammering floated up from downstairs. Had Romein decided to move his wheel inside the mill? Surely not.

No, the sound was coming from outside the door.

Whoever was knocking did not content himself with merely hammering at the door. No, he began to shout in between blows.

"Romein! Madman! Lover!"

And again:

"Romein! Madman! Lover!"

A pause, then:

"I conjure thee! I conjure thee by Rosaline's bright eyes,

By her high forehead and her scarlet lip,

By her fine foot, straight leg and quivering thigh!"

Some swearing, followed by:

"Curse you, Romein, in the Queen's name I come, in answer to your missive!"

More swearing, then a final:

"Then I shall leave the Queen's gift here, but I shall go, for this field-bed is too cold for me to sleep." Something thumped against the door, and the sounds ceased.

Julia set down her sewing and made her way down the stairs. When she threw open the door, there was no sign of the Queen's messenger, except for a leather bag of papers left on the doorstep. The first was a folded letter bearing the royal seal.

Why would the Queen send a gift to a miller, so far from court?

The rain began anew, sheeting in sideways, and Julia was forced to close the door before the whole lower levels became awash. She set the Queen's gift on the kitchen table, and when she heard Romein come inside for the night, she pointed to the bag and said, "This arrived for you. From the Queen, he said, though he also said some scandalous things about a lady named Rosaline."

Romein grinned. "Then it must have been Mercutio! Where is he?"

"When you didn't come in answer to his shouting, he left. He was already gone when I reached the door, but he left this." She lifted the bag and let it thump onto the table.

His eyes lit up. "The Queen sent an

answer!" He ripped through the royal seal as though it was nothing, his eyes scanning the letter before he threw it down and began pulling papers out of the bag. "We were on the right track with the wind wheel. She has sent drawings of wind wheels…nay, wind mills…crusaders found in the Holy Land, and accounts of how one of the southern cities, built actually on the water, if you can believe that, has reclaimed the sea bed to build houses upon, and grow orchards, by pumping out the water and using the salt…it is called Rialto, she says, and they have been doing this for more than a hundred years…"

Julia could scarcely believe it. "You know how to turn salt-sown lands into gardens? Orchards?"

Romein ducked his head. "Well, not yet, but I knew it was possible, and when I have read all of this, that is what we shall do here. And when we are successful, we will repeat the process throughout the lowlands, until the whole country is a garden, as green as you please, and we never need fear the sea or salt water again!"

"And Veluwe? Would it work there, too?" She held her breath, wishing it could be true, yet knowing what she asked was impossible. Salt-scarred land had never been saved before. Never. Unless this Rialto was real…

"I can't see why not. Though the first step would be getting this windmill working, and we are a long way from that…"

"But how will people feed themselves, while their land is still tainted by salt? If nothing will grow…"

Romein grinned. "Ah, but you forget how valuable salt is. We have more here than we could ever need, a veritable mine of the stuff. And those who live inland pay handsomely for it, to preserve meat through the winter. When I sell the salt from my salt works, I make enough coin to pay men to work it for me, and keep meat in the pot for every day. And that is just one small field. If we were to work the whole lowlands…just imagine."

Julia could imagine. If her father heard of it, he would insist she start work at Veluwe immediately, before the Count found out and began to reclaim Gelderland from the sea, too.

"I'd better get back to my sewing, then," she said.

Twenty

Finally, the rain stopped, and a day dawned that was cold and clear, when the sun sent watery rays of light to tempt Julia to step outside. She intended to visit the stables, to see what progress Romein had made with his new wheel, but one of the men from the salt works called, "Lady Julia!"

In a moment, they were all calling greetings and exclaiming over her return, for they'd heard word from Veluwe that she had gone home to her father.

"Do you mean to mine the salt, as Master

Romein is here, Lady Julia?" one of the men asked.

She racked her brain for his name. Henk, wasn't it? Or was it Jan? No, because Jan, the stouter of the two brothers, stood beside Henk, holding a shovel.

"I would like to. Is harvesting salt harder than harvesting crops?" she asked.

The men laughed.

"Yes, and no, my lady," Henk said. "The harvest is more work, for salt is heavier than wheat, but there is no need to sow or plough the field. If you mean to mine the salt at Veluwe, me and my brothers are ready to come home the moment you give the word. Now, if you wish it, for Master Romein has offered us three weeks' holiday for Yule, and a sack of salt to carry home to our families, as reward for our good work this year."

That was kind of him. She had always given the families of Veluwe gifts of food at Yule, but this year she had precious little to give. Even she lived off Romein's kindness, for he refused to accept any payment for her board and lodging. The saints be praised he hadn't stopped her from sewing the sails for him, or she would be even more deeply in his debt.

But the weight of Henk's words began to sink in. "You mean…you could start turning Veluwe's salt-scarred fields fertile again, so that we could plant crops in the spring?"

The men laughed again. It wasn't malicious – most of them had known her since she'd first arrived at Veluwe, a wide-eyed girl asking questions about everything, for the more she understood, the better she could manage the estate. If anything, they seemed only too happy to help her understand.

"As soon as the ground freezes, there will be nothing simpler, Lady Julia. Master Romein has had the mill ponies working a pump to shift the water from the field, but when the ground freezes, so does the water, and we only have to lift the ice onto barrows and cart it to the river. Once the ice is gone, there is only salt left. With enough men, we could clear several fields before year's end, and if Master Romein will spare us until the spring…perhaps we could even clear the salt from the orchards, too, so you shall have apples again come the autumn."

Julia felt her cheeks flush. These men knew her too well. Amma must have told them how fond she was of apples, for surely no one had seen how she wept at how pitiful this year's harvest was. Scarcely enough to make a single pie or tart, let alone last them the winter. Just the thought of celebrating the new year without any kind of apple cake had been the last straw that sent her scurrying home to her father. Only now, here she was at the mill with Romein, and still there wasn't an apple in sight.

But if she knew next year would be better…

She would take that wager. "Yes. As soon as you are finished working for Master Romein, please get started on the fields at Veluwe. And any salt you mine before year's end is yours to keep."

"You truly are a saint, Lady Julia," Henk said, as the other men nodded their agreement.

She managed a smile at the compliment, but if they knew she was gambling her future and theirs for the hope of an apple cake, they would be more likely to compare her to Eve in the Garden of Eden than any angel or saint.

Twenty-One

It was a week before Christmas when the supply boat finally arrived. Two weeks late, and Romein had begun to fear that he would be forced to spend the entire Yule season at the mill instead of at home with his family. So when he heard the sailors' shouts from the river as they tied up, he dropped his tools and raced outside to see for himself.

The men from the salt works pitched in to help unload, and they were soon trooping in and out of the mill, carrying sacks and barrels enough to see him through the winter. Julia stood just outside the door, staring, but then one of the men ducked his head and said something to her, and she answered him with a smile.

Curious, Romein moved closer.

Another man ducked his head as he stepped over the threshold with a sack over each shoulder. "Lady Julia," he said.

"Henk," she said.

These must be men from Veluwe, that she knew them by name. Yet they called her Lady Julia, not miss or mistress, as he would expect of anyone but the Bishop's wife, the lady of the estate herself. But Julia had said she had no husband, and he did not believe she had lied about that. So if she was not the Bishop's wife, then she must be his daughter. Romein had heard nothing about the Bishop having a daughter, only sons, but he'd also seen how she travelled as a man in company with her brothers, so it made sense that the Bishop wished to protect his only daughter as best he could. Sending her out to Veluwe, where no one would see her, until he meant to marry her off to cement some alliance or other.

That must be why she was headed home —
answering a summons from her father, to
obtain a husband she did not yet have.

His heart ached at the thought of Julia,
handed over to some old man, like a Yule gift.
Stuck in a loveless marriage, her brilliant mind
confined to the great house of some lord as
she was forced to lie with him, and bear his
heirs. Just the thought of some stranger
touching her…undressing her, caressing her,
slaking his lust with her, when she deserved to
be loved, and worshipped, and cherished…

God, what he would give to be allowed to
do those things to her. For her, to her, with
her willing consent, a joyous smile
and…and…

At least Rosaline had chosen that fate. Julia
had been exiled to Veluwe, and now she faced
a worse punishment on her return. And for
what crime? That of being born a woman, a
daughter to that ruthless Bishop, instead of a
son.

"I have strict instructions from your mother
to stuff you into a barrel and carry you home,
if you are not willing to leave the mill and your

projects," the captain of the boat said.

Romein looked up, startled out of his dark thoughts about Julia. "What threats did my mother issue this time?"

Captain Balthasar grinned. "That I should eat nothing but apple cakes, washed down with cider, until spring. The apple harvest has been unusually bountiful this year, and we've eaten them until we were sick, and still the barrels are overflowing. If I am not mistaken, there will be plenty of apples among your supplies, too. The cider will not be ready until the new year, so the cider kegs will be ballast in the boat when I bring you home."

Romein rubbed his hands together. A jug of spiced cider in the evening was just how he liked to end a hard day's work. If he could share it with Julia…

But what to do with her, while he was gone? He could hardly leave her here alone in the mill for Yule. She might not be able to ride yet, which meant she could go neither home nor back to Veluwe, but there was no reason she could not come with him to Valkhof.

Well, other than the fact that she was the

Bishop's daughter, and not exactly a welcome guest in the house of Count Montague of Gelderland.

Romein gritted his teeth. This feud be damned. The Bishop and his father could hate each other until their dying day, but Julia was his guest. By the laws of hospitality, he was bound to protect her from the moment they shared a meal together, and he would make sure his father did the same. Even if he had to serve Julia bread and wine with his own hands at his father's table, so that his father was bound by the same laws.

His mind made up, Romein marched up to Julia. "I'm going to spend Yule with my family in Valkhof, and closing up the mill. The men are going home to their families, too. Will you come with me, as my guest?"

For a moment, her eyes shone, before her face fell. "You forget that I cannot ride yet. My ribs are not yet healed."

Romein grinned. "Who said anything about riding? We shall be sailing, and I will need you as my guide to make sure we do not sail into any storms, or do anything else stupid."

She stared at him, the sort of look that measured his soul. "I think that if you set your heart on something, stupid or not, not all the angels and saints in heaven combined would be able to stop you, once your mind is made up. Any other man would have given up on this windmill long ago."

He leaned in. "And any other woman would have given me up for a fool even sooner, yet still you sew sails for me. I think you believe in this windmill as much as I do, and you wish to see it work, so that together we can free this land of the watery burden that has weighed it down for so long."

She opened her mouth, ready to retort in kind, then closed it again, as a delicate blush heated her cheeks. She swallowed instead. "I would do anything to save this land."

He believed her.

"But not during Yule, which is a time for feasting and family and I forget what else. So come with me. The windmill will be waiting here on our return, when we come back, refreshed." He held out his hand. "I have not spent Yule with my family for seven years.

They will be so happy to see me, that any guest I bring with me will receive so warm a welcome, you will think they are your family, too." He fought to keep a straight face, for the thought of the Bishop's daughter as family to the Count…

But oh how he wished she could be…

Slowly, Julia gave a nod, and slipped her hand into his. "I hope I do not regret this."

So did Romein. For if his family found out who she was…

"If you wish to leave, you have only to seek out the good Captain Balthasar here, and he will take you home directly," Romein said. "Isn't that right, Captain Balthasar?"

For a moment, the captain hesitated, directing a searching look at Julia. When he did not appear to find what he looked for, he bowed. "It would be my pleasure to transport your lady anywhere she wishes."

Romein opened his mouth to admit Julia was not his, and might never be, but Balthasar would surely demand an explanation. An explanation he dared not give. Instead, he sighed. "We'd better pack some clothing, then, for they depart as soon as the salt is loaded, and the men are making quick work of that."

Julia nodded and led the way inside. Romein could do naught else but follow.

Twenty-Two

It had been seven years since Romein had seen Valkhof, but the city had changed irrevocably in that time. Great earthen walls had sprung up around the buildings, towering above the deep canals that now ringed it round. It took him a moment to recognise it as the embodiment of the plans he'd sent his father, the first year he'd been at Queen Molina's court. Then several more minutes, surveying the surrounding fields, before he was certain.

"It worked!" he crowed.

Captain Balthasar and his men took no

notice, too busy sailing the boat, but Julia shot him a questioning glance.

"It was my first plan to drain the flooded fields, to keep the towns safe," he explained. "High earth walls to keep the water in or out, and deep channels carved into the earth to hold more water. You see…"

She nodded as he pointed out the details as he noticed them, her gaze following his finger here, there and everywhere. He knew her well enough to be sure she wasn't just feigning interest. He suspected it would only be a moment or two before she asked…

"Is that what you intend to do to the lands around Elst and Veluwe?"

Ah, her first question.

"It is, though the ground is lower there than here at Valkhof, so the salt has had longer to sink into the soil, and the water lingers for longer. It is around Veluwe that we must start to tame the waters, before it can spread to the rest of the country, but that will take years, so in the meantime, earth ramparts around the cities and towns are the best defence we have…"

They discussed how such walls might be used in Veluwe as the boat docked, and they walked through the winding streets up to Father's house. His family were at dinner when they arrived, so he had only a moment to stare at the sea of faces and mumble something along the lines of, "This is Julia. She's helping me convert the mill from horse power to wind," before he was pulled into the nearest pair of arms for a hug.

Julia, too, was subjected to the same treatment, passed from hand to hand until seats were found for them on a bench at the end of one of the tables. Loaded trenchers landed on the table before them, and they were expected to do little more than eat, drink, smile and nod, as the conversation continued around them.

Twenty-Three

Julia had never seen so many people in one place. Her father had never allowed her to attend a feast so full of people, and family meals were a quiet affair, attended only by her parents, her brothers, and herself. This was Romein's family – just his family, not their bannermen. His brothers and their wives, nieces and nephews, plus his parents. This great hall had no dais, for all the tables were equal…well, perhaps not the ones where the children sat, and there seemed to be a great number of those.

She'd half expected someone to ask her for details about Romein's windmill, for she had been introduced as his assistant in the enterprise, but no one seemed to care. Even Romein's explanations were cut off, still half-formed, as the only thing his relatives wanted to ask about was what life was like at court.

She listened, rapt, as Romein told them the story she had not had the courage to ask for.

He'd spent the last seven years serving Queen Molina at court, as a sort of apprentice to her artificer, Master Zimmerman. Where a normal queen had ladies in waiting, Queen Molina had only female apprentices, which Romein had evidently told his family about in his letters home. That explained why no one questioned her introduction as his assistant – they all thought her one of the Queen's ladies. Julia only wished it were true. To think, she might have been learning how to save Veluwe instead of watching it sink beneath the waters, unable to stop it.

But there were too many people around to allow Romein to monopolise the conversation long. The talk turned to this year's harvest, and how hard the winter might be, whether there would be flooding or snow, and when, and whether the talk of a new crusade would be endorsed by the Pope...her head spun by the time someone showed her to her chamber, where she found her things waiting for her, and she fell into bed, asleep almost before her head hit the pillow.

The next day, she was dragged off to help the other women decorate the house with pine boughs, holly and mistletoe, then to help the children make gifts for everyone for New Year's Day. This mostly involved having her hands sticky with honey, and flour dusting her gown, as the scents of spices and dried fruits made her mouth water.

Luckily, a maid carried away her soiled gowns every night, and returned with them, dry and fresh, several days later, without a word of admonishment. Amma would not be so forgiving, but then there seemed to be so many more people here than she'd ever seen at Veluwe.

At the New Year's Eve feast, a grander affair than any she'd attended yet, Julia was pulled aside by Lady Mona, Romein's mother, the one woman whose name she didn't dare forget.

"We have a tradition here, that I'm sure my son remembers, though he has been away from home for too long. Ever since he was old enough to join the feast, his favourite food has been the oil cakes the cook only makes for the new year. And because they are his favourite, and he was the youngest of all his brothers, the tradition is that he must have the first one, before anyone else."

Julia nodded. Her brothers had spoiled her, too, often bringing her choice morsels from the feasts her father had not allowed her to attend.

"The cook is making them now. I think the best way to remind Romein of this tradition would be if you brought the first dish of cakes out, instead of one of the maids, and set it before him."

As though she were one of the maids? Is that what his family thought of her? Julia wasn't sure what to say. She knew her gowns were not the fashionable silks surely worn at court, but…

"New year is when we unite the old and the new. We celebrate the past, and look to the future. So for past traditions to be carried into the future by one who will be an important part of Romein's future…" Mona smiled. "My son cares a great deal for you. He would not have brought you here if he did not. It is true, then, that you and he have plans for the future together?"

Of course they did. Together, they would make a working windmill and lift the curse of flooding from the lowlands, Veluwe and Gelderland alike. "Yes…"

"Then please, go to the kitchen and bring the platter of cakes that the cook will give you."

Julia tried to catch Romein's eye, but he was too busy talking to one of his brothers to notice. Sighing, she resolved to do as Lady Mona bade her. It was hardly the first time she'd been asked to pretend to be a servant. The whole journey to Veluwe, Thibault had insisted on her being his cupbearer. At least Romein would have the good manners to thank her, instead of spilling ale down her tunic.

Even in a house she did not know well, Julia only had to follow her nose to find the kitchen.

"You are young Romein's lady?"

Julia blinked.

The cook emerged from the shadows, her eyes intent on her. In her hand, she held a spoon so large it could have been used to stir a cauldron…or cudgel someone to death.

Swallowing, Julia said, "Lady Mona said I should come and fetch the oil cakes?"

The cook grinned. "First, you must taste them, and when you are married, you must send your cook to me, so that I can teach her how to make them. Some stuff them with raisins, but mine are always sweeter, for the secret is fresh made apple sauce."

Apple? Julia's mouth watered. It had been too long since she'd tasted one. To think they had enough here to make apple sauce…and use them in cakes…

"Or you could tell me how to make them, and I can write it down, and share that with my cook," Julia said. For there was no guarantee that she would ever marry, or come back…

The cook looked her up and down. "So you are a scholar, too, reading and writing like young Romein? No wonder he has taken such a fancy to you. Trust him to find the only pretty lady scholar in the world."

Julia was saved the need to answer, for the cook disappeared into the smoky darkness then, reappearing a long moment later bearing a bowl of steaming balls that smelled divine. Cinnamon and apple and honey, oh…she nearly cried as she reached for the bowl.

The cook hugged the bowl to her breast. "They are too hot yet, mind. I shall set them on the table to cool a moment. Then you may have one without burning your tongue."

But leaving Julia alone with temptation itself was even worse. The cakes steamed, sending up tendrils of scent that begged her to take just a bite. Eve in Eden could not have resisted. Julia stretched out her hand…

Only to have it smacked away.

Twenty-Four

Curse it, he could smell apple and cinnamon. He knew the cook was making oil cakes, but his mother would not cease her chatter and allow him to go off in search of them. Yes, he might have been absent for seven years, and one of his nephews had likely taken his place as the first to eat the new year cakes, but he was home now, and by all that was holy, he would not yield this year.

Mother paused for breath, and Romein blurted out, "Pray excuse me," before he bolted away, intent on reaching the kitchens.

And there they were, sitting on a table alone, calling his name.

Until a small hand reached out of the darkness to steal one.

Romein's fury knew no bounds. Who dared steal the first cake? Whoever's son this was, he deserved to be whipped.

Romein smacked the boy's hand away.

Only to hear a startled cry that belonged to no boy.

"Oh God, Julia, forgive me!" He seized her hand in his own, stroking the reddened skin he had dared to strike. "Please, permit me to smooth my rough touch with a tender kiss." He did not wait for permission, but pressed his lips to her hand. He should have stopped at one kiss, but he could not. Dared not, until he had covered her injured hand in kisses and still he begged for her forgiveness.

There was only one thing to do. He seized the nearest cake and held it out to her. "Every year, I have broken and eaten the first cake to bless the new year. I came to bring them to you, so that we might share it, and the new year's blessing might fall on our...fall on our..."

Her fingers grazed his as she took the cake, and bit it in half, then held out the other half to him. Then the taste must have hit her tongue, for she cast her eyes heavenward, as if in prayer.

One look at her parted lips, and it was not prayer or cake Romein thought of, though the taste of apple and cinnamon was still on her lips, and the sweetness of honey lingered on her tongue. Though he knew it was surely the greatest of sins, he leaned in to kiss this angel again.

Twenty-Five

The apple cake was everything the cook had said, and more. A bite of heaven, surely. Julia closed her eyes, savouring the taste. No wonder Romein had defended the cakes so fiercely. Having tasted, now she would fight with equal ferocity, should anyone threaten to take what was hers.

Warmth brushed her lips, and for a moment, she thought he meant to feed her another cake, but this smelled of spiced cider, far richer than any cake.

"Yes," she breathed, a moment before his

lips touched hers, and he kissed her. This was no kiss of peace, over in a moment and forgotten a moment later. No, this was one stolen breath after another, a dance of lips and tongues and air that sent her head whirling and her heart drumming while pipes skirled in her belly and her legs turned to water that would scarcely hold her weight any more.

She gazed into his eyes, and for a moment, she saw forever. She would be lost forever if she did not go now.

So she fled, forcing her unwilling legs to carry her out of the kitchen, out of the house, and down to the river where Captain Balthasar and his boat would take her to safety.

Twenty-Six

His arms wanted to pull her closer, but when she resisted, he knew he had to let her go. And she flew into the night, as if borne by angels' wings. Angels saving her from him, for nothing good could come of Romein, son of Montague, kissing Julia Capet. For to ask for her hand would be to hand his own life over, in his foe's debt.

But for her, perhaps it would be worth the cost...

He longed to chase after her, to beg her forgiveness once more, but he dare not. His mother would come looking for him, and there were the damned cakes to break in the new year. Romein closed his eyes.

He would find Julia later, when his ardour had cooled, and apologise. He might blame the cider for heating his blood, but he knew it had nothing to do with the cider, and everything to do with her.

The rest of the night passed in a blur, until he could excuse himself to retire. It was noon before he rose, only to find no sign of Julia. Even her clothes were gone.

Evening was falling by the time he recovered his wits enough to head down to the dock, where he found Balthasar, tying up his boat.

"Have you seen her?" Romein begged.

"Your bird has flown home. The last I saw of her, she was crossing the bridge to Elst, headed for Veluwe," Balthasar said. "But I fear you will not catch her before she reaches the Bishop's lands."

No, but he must follow her anyway. "Send word when you are ready to sail again, and take me with you," Romein said.

Balthasar laughed. "My men have sailed all night, and most of the day, too. We must rest, and eat, but when we sail, we shall not leave without you, for if I am not mistaken, she is still your lady love."

Romein prayed the captain was right.

Twenty-Seven

"Amma!" Julia shouted as she led Epona through the gates of Veluwe. "I am…can you…help me…" She could scarcely stand, after loading Epona with food from the mill. She'd left Romein the contents of her coin purse, which would more than pay for what she'd taken, and then walked all the way, leading Epona.

And now, she could not…could not…

The ground swooped up to meet her.

Twenty-Eight

Julia awoke in her own bed, with a chill in the air that berated her for not sending warning, so that a fire might be lit to chase away the chill before she arrived. She sighed.

She should not have kissed him. She should not have enjoyed it so. And, most of all, she should not have run away. No, a sensible woman would have slapped him for taking such liberties.

Never mind that she had liked those liberties very much.

She shouldn't have…

Oh, no, she most certainly should not have fallen in love with the miller, for her father would never allow them to marry.

Unless…well, his family had certainly not been poor. He might be the youngest son, but he had the ear of the Queen. Perhaps…

She dressed and headed down to the kitchen, to see if there was any breakfast. There was no one but Amma, pulling a tray of steaming apple cakes out of the oven. Not quite as fragrant as the ones last night, for there was no cinnamon left, nor oil, but there were apples and honey and flour, and it would be enough.

"Trust you to bring a whole barrel of apples, but not enough flour to last the week," Amma said tartly.

Julia couldn't help but laugh. After lifting the barrel onto Epona's back, she was lucky to have managed to lift anything else at all. "We can ask the miller. He will sell us more."

"Which miller?" Amma asked.

"The one whose mill lies beside the river, across the bridge to Elst," Julia said. The one who kissed like an angel, who she very much wished to taste again.

"The miller there died some years ago, soon after you arrived," Amma said.

"There is a new one now, who recently took the place over," Julia said.

"You mean young Master Romein, the youngest son of Count Montague of Gelderland? He would sooner sell us to the devil than trade with us for flour."

Julia's heart turned to ice. "The son of who?"

"Montague. The son of your great enemy, the Count of Gelderland."

No. He could not be. The Count of Gelderland was…she couldn't have been…in the richest house in Valkhof, which could only belong to the Count…

Oh God.

She had fallen in love with the Count's son.

Her first and only love, sprung from the loins of the man her father hated most. If she had but known…yet now she knew, it was too late. Fate must truly be laughing at her, for falling in love with a loathed enemy.

<h1 style="text-align: center;">Twenty-Nine</h1>

"Lady Julia, you have a visitor," Amma said as she set down a platter containing Julia's noon meal.

Her heart lifted at the thought that it must be Romein, for surely no one else could possibly be travelling on such a cold day. Then her heart plummeted just as rapidly as it had risen, as she realised Romein did not know she had returned to Veluwe, or that she lived here at all.

No one visited Veluwe, for fear of the Bishop's wrath.

So who, then, could her visitor be?

"Send the visitor in, then," Julia said.

"Are you sure?"

For Amma to question her was a strange enough occurrence to give Julia pause. Perhaps it was Romein, who had learned her whereabouts from Henk or one of the other men, who were even now digging the salt out of her orchards.

"Would you advise me to send him away, then?" Julia asked.

Amma wrinkled her nose. "It is not my place to advise you in such things. Nor do I think that you would be successful in sending him away. The man has arrived in full armour, with sword unsheathed, and none of my boys are much of a match for an armoured knight."

Not Romein, then, for he owned no such armour, and she had never seen him carry a sword, let alone wield one.

"Did he give his name?"

"Sir Paris, I think. It was difficult to be sure, as he has his visor down and his voice was much muffled by all that metal."

Julia sighed. A man who entered her home

with his sword drawn did not mean to invoke the laws of hospitality. She'd be a fool to let him in at all. "So he is in the bailey now?"

"Yes, as all the doors are barred. He shouts your name, and demands to see you."

And likely had no intention of leaving until he had seen her. Very well, she would be seen. Julia rose from the table and headed up to the balcony. She glimpsed Henk and his brothers, hard at work, but didn't dare stop to watch them. Instead, she turned toward the bailey, and the noisy knight.

He strode about the bailey, muttering unintelligible things, and hammering on various doors that did not open. His nervous horse shied away from him, looking longingly out the gate, but the creature did not dare flee for freedom.

Julia allowed herself a small smile. Epona would not be so timid. The mare would have lost patience with the man long since, and tried to trample him. How her hooves would fare against armoured plate, Julia wasn't sure, but Epona would have at least put some dents in such shiny armour before retiring from the fight.

"Who are you?" Julia called.

The knight stopped and looked around. When he didn't see her, he shouted something unintelligible and hammered on the tower door again.

Julia leaned over the balcony. "Take your helmet off, so that I might actually hear you. I asked for your name, knight."

Finally, the knight looked up and saw her.

It took him a moment, and many muttered words that were very likely unfit for a lady's ears, before he managed to wrench the helmet off. "For God's sake, Julia, let me in. I bring news from your father."

The man only had one eye. She stared at the patch that covered his deformity, then at the rest of his scarred face, before she finally recognised him. "Thibault?" she asked.

"Of course it's me, silly girl. Who else would your father send?"

William or Aran, for her brothers were surely more trustworthy than her bastard cousin. And…was he missing an ear, too? Now he truly resembled the tom cat back home, with his battle scars. Prince of Cats, indeed.

"But that is not the name you gave to my housekeeper just now."

"We are family, so you may call me by name. But a mere servant…" Thibault curled his lip in disgust. "They must address me as Sir Thibault of Paris, renowned tourney champion."

Well, that explained where he'd been for the last seven years, and the scars. "What are you doing here?"

"Your father sent me. The Count of Gelderland has grown wealthy of late, with rumours of a new salt mine in the lowlands. Your father wishes a strong hand to hold Veluwe against whatever forces he might send against it. For there are plenty of knights for hire who would happily take his money, and more besides."

It took Julia a moment to work out how that involved Thibault. "So, you're here for my protection."

"Of course. As a renowned tourney champion, your father knew I was the best man for the job."

One knight against an army of mercenaries, or even a small company of knights with both their eyes…unless Thibault was a far better fighter than she remembered, he could not offer more protection than the walls of Veluwe. They had only to close the gates.

"Thibault…" She had to find the right words so that he would not see the facts as an insult.

"Sir Thibault. Though I suppose you may call me simply Thibault when we are alone together. We are to be married, after all."

"What?"

He puffed out his chest. "Your father will arrive in a week, with more men to defend you, but he expects us to be married by then. You must organise a feast, of course, for that is women's work, and I shall be too busy defending this place and taking stock of my new estate to bother with such unimportant things. I insist there must be suckling pig, and roast venison, and a fat goose, for it is hardly a wedding feast without them."

Julia's blood boiled. They did not have pigs

or deer or geese anywhere in Veluwe, unless Thibault counted as a goose, for thinking she'd ever agree to marry him.

"What makes you think I would marry you?" she said.

"Your father, of course. He promised me your hand in marriage when you are old enough. Why else would I have escorted you all the way out here when you were a girl? You were too young for marriage then, your father said, and he said I must wait. But now…now he says you are ready, and you shall be mine, as you were always meant to be."

She hadn't eaten more than a bite of her midday meal, but now she wanted to vomit up everything in her belly at the prospect of allowing Thibault to touch her, let alone marry her. She swallowed back bile. This was no time to lose her head, or her breakfast, either. She had to think. "That is…glad tidings indeed. But surely my father would want to be present at the marriage of his only daughter, and feasts take time to prepare. I shall…send word to the priest at Saint Martin's church to await my father's arrival, for on that day, God willing, we shall be married."

She'd rather marry one of Romein's mill ponies than Thibault. This was madness. Her father could not possibly give his only daughter to a penniless bastard, with no honour to his name except a tourney title. Unless that was Father's intention — to buy Thibault's loyalty with her maidenhead, so the man would be more likely to do her father's bidding. Perhaps her father intended him to fight and die for Veluwe, while taking her home, far from the conflict, so that when she was widowed, he might marry to her to a more worthy man…

In a week, she would find out, for she could ask her father himself. In a week, she still might have to marry the man. Julia suppressed a shudder. She would have to formulate a plan to avoid such a fate, and she only had a few days to do so.

But in the meantime…

She sighed. "Fine. Take off your armour, and you can come inside. We can post guards at the gates, who will give us fair warning if any of the Count's men approach, so you have time to put it all on again."

Thibault beamed. "You shall make a fine wife, cousin. See that there is goose for dinner. If I am to be the lord of the manor, my table should reflect my station."

His table would be far more sparse than he expected, what with it being winter after a poor harvest and all. But there was some goose confit in the cellar, which might satisfy him for at least a little while. God forbid she have to feed him for more than a week.

Because if there was one thing she knew for certain, it was that she would rather die than become Thibault's wife.

Thirty

The pile of coins on Romein's kitchen table told him Julia had come to the mill, and taken supplies with her. Judging by the quantity of what was gone, she could not have travelled far – Veluwe, most likely, just as Captain Balthasar had surmised.

Father had been generous, loading the ship with enough food to see Romein well into spring, but Romein knew that was only a fraction of the value of the salt he had given his father during his time here. Which would multiply tenfold once he had the windmill working…

And for that, he needed Julia.

He would find her, apologise for his foolish, cider-fuelled kisses, and offer her anything and everything she could possibly want to come back to the mill and help him. Because only together could they save the lowlands.

He loaded up two of the mill ponies with some of the choicest foods Mother had sent, including a basket of oil cakes, left over from the new year feast, and set off across the bridge to Elst.

Thirty-One

Romein had never seen Veluwe before, but he'd imagined something more like his father's house in Valkhof. Not this strange wooden fort, walled in on all sides like a miniature city, with a tower rising up in the middle, overlooking the lands it ruled. There was only one gate, and it was closed.

So Romein strolled up to the gate and knocked.

"Who goes there?"

For a moment, Romein considered actually giving the guard his name, and his father's, too.

For it was no secret – Julia surely knew the truth, for what reason would she have had to run from his father's house except finding out she'd been kissed by her enemy?

It could not have been the kiss itself, Romein told himself. It couldn't have. Or she would have pushed him away or frozen or something, other than kiss him back. And she had most definitely kissed him back.

Or maybe it was the kiss. Maybe he should have practiced more when he was at court, instead of mooning after Rosaline. Then, he might still be in Valkhof with Julia, sharing a cup of mulled cider in the warmth of his family's hall, as he worked up the courage to ask her for her hand.

Instead of standing outside the gates of her castle, praying that they would open. He glanced at the mill ponies, labouring under full loads. He had no intention of making them carry such weights home again. "I brought supplies. Delicacies for Lady Julia's table."

"What sort of delicacies?" The man peered over the palisade. His cloak pin caught the light, and Romein blinked in surprise.

Of course, he should not have been surprised at all to see the Bishop's family crest on the man, for Julia was a Capet, after all, and the fleur-de-lis her family's emblem. But he'd only seen such a cloak pin once, and the man who wore it had been the oaf who threw him in the river.

Romein squinted up at him. The young man he remembered must have been in many battles since then, to own a face so scarred. But his voice had not changed.

"I don't rightly know. My master told me to deliver the food to the castle for the lady, and I don't ask questions. Just do my job," Romein said, trying to slow down his speech to sound like one of the salt workers. "The miller said he'd give me an extra loaf of bread if I returned the ponies before nightfall, though, so if you'd be so kind, sir, and open the gate…"

The oaf waved to someone behind him, and the gates swung open.

No one helped him unload the horses, but Romein did not mind much. Everyone seemed to eye him with suspicion — first the oaf up on the battlements, and then the grey-haired woman in the kitchen. Julia's cook, he presumed.

Romein pressed the basket of oil cakes into the cook's hands. "For Lady Julia, with my best wishes for a prosperous new year," he said.

The cook's eyes narrowed. "And who might I tell her they are from?"

Romein bowed low. "From a friend, who wishes her every happiness, and hopes that this gift will at least make her smile."

The cook seized his hand. "If you are truly her friend, then perhaps you can help her. Come to the orchard after dark, for the lady surveys the progress on the salt works every evening from her balcony. If you would have her see you…"

Romein grinned. "I would love nothing more. Thank you, mistress."

He hurried to unload the rest of his cargo, before hustling the horses up to the village, where he knew Henk and his brothers lived.

When the sun set, and the men arrived home, they invited him to join them for dinner, but Romein declined, saying he had business up at the castle with Lady Julia.

The brothers exchanged glances, before Henk said, "The best way to reach Lady Julia, with that fool guarding the gates, is to take one of the ladders in the orchard, and set it upon one of the snowdrifts beside the walls. It might not quite reach the balcony, but it will get you close enough to exchange words with her, without the fool knowing anything about it."

Romein clapped him on the shoulder. "You are a good man, and loyal to Lady Julia. I'll make sure she knows it."

"Oh, she knows all right. We are her people, and no Count or Bishop will sway us from her, not while she still draws breath."

"Then you will not tell..." What was the oaf's name? He should remember it, but he could not...oh! "You will not tell Thibault who I am, or that we have spoken?"

Henk spat twice on the ground. "There's for Thibault and that's for his airs and graces. He's the Bishop's brother's bastard, and no better than the rest of us. It is only out of respect for Lady Julia that we do not run him right off her lands. The only time he deigns to look or speak to us is to complain about where we put the snow when we dig the salt from her fields. Thrice he has told us to stop, for he dislikes seeing bare earth where he thinks there should be white snow. But we are here on Lady Julia's orders, restoring her fields, and we will not stop unless the command comes from her lips alone."

Romein's heart dared to hope. "So she still wants to save the lowlands from the salt?" Perhaps she did not hate him, then, if she still shared his plans.

"She wants Veluwe to be green again, as it was in her mother's day, just like the fields around the mill. She wants the trees to bear fruit, and for the cows to have fresh pasture and…is there a saint of growing things, Master Romein? For if there is not, then I am certain that when she takes her place in heaven, that saint will be her."

If not before she'd saved the lowlands, then definitely after, Romein reflected. But he merely bowed his thanks to the man, and headed back to the castle.

<h1 style="text-align:center;">Thirty-Two</h1>

The wind was cold, so Julia shut the balcony doors. All right, the doors also muffled the sound of Thibault's voice as he shouted at someone in the bailey, so she didn't have to listen to him, but now the doors were shut, she did not want to open them again. Henk and the other men were making good progress on the orchard – she'd glimpsed the dark soil that lay hidden beneath the salt before she'd retreated inside.

Amma came up the stairs, carrying a basket. It was early for dinner, but Julia did not have much appetite these days anyway. "What is it today?" she asked.

Amma set the basket on the table. "A gift from the miller, who asks only that you venture out onto the balcony to see how work is going in the orchard, after the sun sets."

"Which miller?" Julia asked suspiciously. Surely she could not mean…

"The miller who knows it is death to him if he should set foot on your lands, yet he delivered the basket to me with his own hands, and begged me to give them to you."

Romein. It had to be Romein.

She pulled the cloth covering from the basket and nearly cried at the contents. The basket was full of oil cakes, no longer hot and crisp from the pan, but soft and richer smelling, almost as if the cinnamon had infused the dough since they were first baked.

Julia couldn't resist. She bit into one, and it tasted just as good as the first one Romein had given her.

"Did he say anything else?" For if he had come here, he knew who she was, as she knew who his family was.

"Only that he desires your happiness, and wishes you to smile."

Oh, what she would give for happiness, instead of a blighted future with Thibault as her husband. Try as she might, she had not been able to work out a way to avoid it.

But it would warm her heart to see Romein again, and know that he did not hate her.

"The sun has set, Lady Julia."

Julia jerked out of her reverie. "Thank you, Amma. I shall…retire early tonight, instead of coming down to supper. I will bolt the doors after you go."

Amma dropped a curtsey. "Very good, my lady. I will see that your guest has plenty of strong wine to drink, so that he sleeps well tonight."

Julia nodded. She waited for Amma to depart, then bolted her bedchamber door, before throwing open the door to the balcony.

It was cold and dark out there. She wrapped a cloak about her shoulders and reached for a lamp before she dared step through the door.

"Soft! What light through yonder window breaks? It is the east, and Julia is the sun!"

Julia whirled, to find him crouched in the shadows beside the door. "Romein?"

"It is, my lady."

"What are you doing here?"

"Admiring your beauty, for it has been several days since I last beheld it. Your eyes outshine two of the fairest stars in the heaven…"

"Oh, don't be silly. How did you get here?"

"With night's cloak to hide me, and love's light wings to fly over these walls, for no stony limits or your kinsman could keep me out."

She held her lantern out, looking toward the orchard. "You took one of the ladders, set it upon a snowdrift so that it leaned against the walls, and…you cannot be here. Thibault is here, and if he sees you, he will murder you, to finish the job he did not do all those years ago."

"I have not come for him, but for you." He rose and entered her chamber, for all the world like he had every right to be there. "Did you like my gift? Beneath the cakes, there is some parchment. I wrote down the recipe, for my mother's cook insisted I do so."

Julia closed her eyes. "Your mother, the Countess of Gelderland?"

Romein nodded, grinning around a mouthful of cake. "The wife of Count Montague of Gelderland, my father. As you are Lady Julia Capet, only daughter of the Bishop of Maastricht. Mortal enemies in name only, for I cannot hate you, and I believe you might have some fond feelings for me, if only because I bring you gifts. Including a barrel of strong wine that will see your new gate guard sleep soundly tonight, or so your cook promises me."

Her gate guard. Oh, if that was all he was. "My father means to make me marry him. He will be here within the week, to preside over my wedding to that man. He fears your father, and the mercenaries he might hire with his new-found wealth from his new salt mine."

"Your father would not be so cruel."

Their eyes met, full of knowing at that lie. The Bishop's cruelty knew no bounds. He would even sacrifice her, if he must.

"I will not allow it."

Julia laughed. "I don't see how you can stop

him. I don't see how I can stop him, either, though I have spent every waking moment trying to work out how I might."

"Marry me instead."

Her heart soared. Oh, if only she could. "My father would never allow it."

"Then do not wait for his permission. We will go to Elst tonight, to the church of Saint Martin, and there, we will entreat Father Laurence to marry us. Those God has joined together, no man may separate."

"Romein…" She had never wished for anything more. Never wanted anything quite as much as she wanted this. And yet…

"Marry me, Julia. Be my wife, and together we shall build windmills and salt mines, and save the lowlands from floods."

She had to laugh. Only Romein could talk of windmills and marriage in the same sentence. "And what of love?"

"If you will permit me, I shall show you more love in one kiss, than in all the arranged marriages your father could devise. The moment my lips touch yours, you shall know the depth of my devotion is greater than the ocean, wider than the sea, more constant than the waves that pound the shore…" A faint flush coloured his cheeks. "Perhaps we should not speak of such things yet. At least not until we are married. If you will have me."

The Bishop's obedient daughter considered saying no, but Julia was more than one man's daughter. She was the Lady of Veluwe, chatelaine of these lands, responsible for its people, and the mistress of her own destiny.

"And if I have you, what of my father, when he comes with his men to wrest Veluwe from us?" Us. The word seemed to whisper on the wind, of what might be, if she only dared.

"We shall do what he fears most, and hire mercenaries to defend your lands. For they are yours, as they were your mother's, and together we will protect them as no one else has."

"But he is my father. My family. I could not go to war against my own family!"

Romein took her hands in his. "You are a Capet, and I am of Montague. Sworn enemies, already at war. But as my wife, you become a Montague, too. Your family would have you marry Thibault and lose your lands to the rising sea, while mine would ask you to do no more than you mean to do already: rule Veluwe, and keep it safe."

Oh, that she could have such things with but a word, and a small one at that. Finally, Julia dared to hope. "And what of you? What would you have me do?"

Romein grinned. "First, I would have you kiss me, so that I might prove my love for you. Later, after we are married, I would have you share my bed, instead of leaving me to sleep on the floor by the kitchen fire, as I did every night you slept in my box bed at the mill. I would have you in all of the thousand ways it is possible to pleasure a woman, or so the scholars say. There was a book in Queen Molina's library that was written by some sultan's eunuch, and I would delight in demonstrating all that I learned from its pages. Why, you would never want to leave my bed…"

His eyes followed her gaze to her bed, not three steps away.

"How soon may we marry?" Julia asked.

"Tonight, if you wish it. We can climb down

the ladder, and head to Elst."

Her mouth was dry, but other parts of her felt alarmingly wet. Did she want more kisses? Did she want him to share her bed? Did she want…everything he offered?

"Yes," Julia breathed.

Thirty-Three

Waking Father Laurence when they got to Elst took longer than Romein had expected. Both he and Julia yawned in between their vows, and by the time they returned to her balcony, dawn was already breaking.

Yet as his eyes met hers, he wished he could stay.

"Must you go? It is not yet day," Julia said.

Romeo laughed. "The sun's streaks lace the severing clouds in the east. Night's candles are burned out. It is day, or near enough. Do not fret, for night follows day, and our wedding night will come soon enough."

"Not soon enough. Today, I find I hate windows, for mine let day in, and love out," Julia complained.

"The mill has no windows. Meet me there in the hour after dusk, and I shall make you the happiest of brides, I swear it." But he was as tempted as she. "Farewell, farewell…give me but one more kiss, before I descend."

Julia threw her arms about his neck and kissed him, with all the eagerness he could ever wish for. Oh, that night would fall right now…

But no. It was day, and he wanted to finish the windmill before she arrived. And she would need rest, for they would not get much sleep tonight.

He forced himself down the ladder, until his boot sank into snow. Then he allowed himself one last glance up at her, a moment to blow a kiss, before he seized the ladder and was gone.

Thirty-Four

Married. To Romein. No longer a Capet, but a Montague. Julia could scarcely believe it, but one look at Romein on the ladder below her, and she knew it was true.

Then dread's dark wings engulfed her, for as she saw Romein, so far below, for a moment, in dawn's faint light, he appeared too pale, like one dead in the bottom of a tomb.

She whispered a prayer that it was not so. She was a water witch, not a seer.

A soft knock at the door dragged her from the balcony.

"Lady Julia? I brought up fresh water, so you might wash. I shall have breakfast ready directly. Would you like me to bring it up, or will you take it downstairs?"

"I'll come down for breakfast, Amma. Leave the water jug outside the door. I'll just be a moment."

"Very good, my lady." The jug clunked to the floor, before the sound of Amma's footsteps died away.

Julia washed and changed into a new gown, wishing she'd had more time with her husband to enjoy being his wife. But that would come tonight, she promised herself, before she headed down to breakfast.

The kitchen was quiet, filled with the normal morning bustle as Amma and one of her daughters in law made bread and prepared a pot of soup to set on the fire for dinner.

"We are almost out of fish, Lady Julia," Amma said.

"If the weather is fine, I shall take the boat out on the river today, and see what I can catch," Julia said. She could not remember the last time she had sailed, aside from aboard

Captain Balthasar's ship. One day, she must take Romein out on the boat, and teach him to sail.

"The first loaf is ready, my lady. Would you prefer butter or honey?" Nellie asked.

Julia wanted soft cheese, but until they replaced the dairy herd, there would be no fresh milk or cheese. "Honey," she said, for that was a fitting wedding breakfast, surely, on the first day of her honeymoon? Though she should be sharing the meal with her new husband...

On the morrow, she promised herself.

When she'd finished the bread, and washed the honey from her fingers, Julia turned to Amma. "I know we need fish, but how are our other stores? I mean to call by the mill this evening, so I will see what he can spare." She fought to cool the telltale blush threatening to burn her cheeks.

Nellie was too busy setting the new loaves in the oven, but Amma had surely seen. Then again, Amma had known she'd spent the night with Romein, so her cheeks would tell the housekeeper no tales she did not already suspect.

"We have almost no meat left, and the flour is running low. We have enough vegetables to last the week, but not enough to see us until spring. This is the last crock of butter, and while we have hard cheese enough to see us for some weeks yet, I fear it will not be enough if Sir Thibault is our guest for much longer."

From the thinning of Amma's lips, Julia knew she thought even less of Thibault than she herself did. She wished she could find some pity in her for the poor scarred man, but when he behaved like a…

"Julia! Why is there no ham? Or eggs? We are in the country – surely someone can go out and catch a pig or something!" Thibault appeared in the kitchen doorway, his eyes as red as his nose. He'd evidently drunk far too much wine last night, and was still feeling the effects.

Any other morning, she might have tried to placate him. But that was before she knew he'd eaten most of her winter stores, stores she'd bought from Romein. Now she'd married Romein, she refused to support the leech any longer.

"There are no pigs because we slaughtered and salted the last one in the autumn. There is no ham because you have eaten it all. And there are no eggs because chickens do not lay eggs when the days are so short and cold. And even if someone did go into the forest to hunt wild boar, they would need an experienced hunting party, and it would take at least a day or two to bleed and dress the carcass, before it could be cooked. What we have is bread, and some honey. If that is not good enough for you, then I suggest you return to Paris and dine with the other tourney champions. Or, better yet, return to my father, and his plentiful table!"

Pain exploded in her cheek. It took her a moment to realise that Thibault had struck her.

"If you ever speak to me again with such disrespect, my soon to be wife, that is just a taste of what I shall give you in return," Thibault spat. "It is your fault the cellars are so bare here. You have mismanaged this place for so many years, it is no wonder even your peasants do not know the first thing about farming. Why, the first thing I shall do when we are married is teach the peasants to do as they are told, just as you will. There will be no digging up fields covered by snow. No, they shall plough and plant in spring, like sensible people. I might not be a farmer, but even I know that crops sown in the dead of winter will die!"

Julia took a deep breath. Tonight, when he had drunk himself into a stupor, she would have the men carry him out and toss him in the river, just like she'd wanted to do when she'd first arrived in Veluwe. Then they would lock the gates, and never allow him to enter Veluwe again.

Luckily, Thibault stormed out of the kitchen, saving her the need to reply.

"My boys will take him to the nearest pigpen and toss him in tonight, my lady," Amma said softly.

Julia managed a smile, though her jaw ached from Thibault's blow. "And I will promise them a smoked ham as a token of my thanks, when we have one to spare."

Thirty-Five

When Romein reached home, he found Mercutio on his doorstep, whistling.

"What are you doing here?" Romein asked, pushing open the door and gesturing for Mercutio to precede him.

"Her Majesty the Queen sent me, with more designs for your windmill. New vanes and plans for a horizontal instead of a vertical axle, for a windmill is not the same as a waterwheel," Mercutio said, pulling papers out of his satchel. He spread them out on the kitchen table. "Look. Master Zimmerman said you get more power with the different axle, and the vanes." He pointed at the sails.

Romein shook his head. He did not regret his night's work, but he did wish he'd had more sleep, for he needed a clear head to make sense of these new sketches. "I would need an entire tree to make such an axle. I do not have a piece of wood so large. I'd need to take all the mill ponies and the cart into the forest for something like that…" But if it would make for a better windmill, it made sense to do it now, before he put everything together, for he'd only have to take it apart again. Romein swore. "Fine. I shall go woodcutting, but you must stay here, in case Lady Julia comes to visit. Tell her where I am, and what I am doing, and that I shall return as soon as I have what we need."

"Tell the lady that you have gone hunting, and will return soon," Mercutio said. "Now, you would not let a growing boy get hungry while he's waiting, would you?"

Romein sighed. He could do with some breakfast, too. "We have a loaf of yesterday's bread, plenty of butter and honey, and a wheel of soft cheese in the buttery…"

"Any more of that spiced sausage?" Mercutio asked eagerly.

Romein blinked. The half sausage that had been on the table only a moment ago was already gone. "I'll go get another," he said. For a well-fed Mercutio would be more inclined to be polite to Lady Julia when she arrived.

When he'd laid a veritable feast on the table before Mercutio, and swallowed a few bites for himself, Romein headed for the stable, to harness the pony cart. This would be a long day.

Thirty-Six

"Close the gates! Close the gates!" The shout came from Henk, as he raced into the bailey.

Julia hurried down to meet him. "What is wrong? Are we in under attack?"

Henk and Jan waited until they'd barred the gates before they turned to answer her. "Not any more. Sir Shouts-A-Lot has just come down to the orchard, ranting and raving about the proper way to plant crops. When we told him we were mining salt, not planting anything, he pitched a fit. Called us traitors and fools and all manner of unpleasant things. So

Jan here told him it was all according to the miller's instructions, for the miller had been mining salt for months in his own fields. Sir Shouts-A-Lot said some even more unpleasant things about Master Romein, before rushing inside to put his armour on. Then he rode out the gates, swearing to teach that upstart miller – his words, not mine, Lady Julia – a lesson in manners."

"But why shut the gates? Surely you should be riding full speed to the mill, to warn Romein!"

Henk shook his head. "Master Romein can take care of himself, Lady Julia. He does sword practice every morning, just like you'd expect of a knight. Not like Sir Shouts-A-Lot, lazing in bed every morning and drinking late into the night, and shouting at people every hour in between." He winked. "When that lazy knight comes running back here from the beating Master Romein will give him, he'll find the gates closed and no welcome waiting. Mistress Amma said she would boil a pot of water and tip it over the palisades if he tries to break down the gate."

Julia wasn't sure whether to laugh or cry at that. But Romein. She could not let him face Thibault in full armour alone. Romein didn't even carry a sword. It was all well and good that he knew how to use one, but if he didn't have one on him and Thibault attacked him while he was defenceless — which she fully believed an honourless bastard would do — Romein would have no chance.

She would not lose her husband to Thibault again. Last time, she'd been too shocked to stop Thibault, but now…now she wished to strike a blow of her own.

Thirty-Seven

The next time Romein needed a beam this big, he swore to himself, he would pay a woodcutter to bring it to him. It was either that or buy a bigger cart, and horses who were used to having big lengths of timber hanging off the back of it. He'd have to give the mill ponies several apples apiece when he reached the mill, and in only a few hours, Julia would arrive…

Romein quickened his step at the thought of his bride, wed but not yet enjoyed. Oh, such pleasure would he give her, so that she did not regret for a moment choosing to marry him.

He left the new axle outside the barn, then unharnessed the horses and put the cart away. He thought he heard raised voices, and headed for the mill, where the words became clearer.

"He's not here, I tell you. He's gone hunting. I'm merely the Queen's messenger, come to bring him a letter from Her Majesty." That was Mercutio's voice. Judging by his tone, he'd repeated this tale several times, and was growing desperate that his interrogator did not believe the simple truth.

Romein hurried up to the house. Whoever was looking for him was about to find him.

"Sir! You will call me Sir!" an unfamiliar voice roared.

Mercutio was one of the Queen's wards, a prince in all but name, much like Isaak. What title he held when he became a man, Romein did not know, but he would definitely outrank any knight.

"You are a rude brute, Sir, and no mistake!" Mercutio said.

Romein rounded the corner just in time to see Thibault, in full plate armour, punch

Mercutio. The boy went down, his head striking the ground hard, and he did not rise.

Romein broke into a run, dropping to his knees beside Mercutio. "Are you hurt?" he asked.

Mercutio grinned, but blood stained his teeth, and his eyes would not seem to focus. "Aye, a scratch, a scratch. 'Tis not so deep, but 'tis enough to scratch a man to death. A braggart, a rogue, a villain…a plague on both your horses!" He wagged his finger at Thibault's horse.

The creature reared up, as if struck, and galloped off.

Mercutio shifted his finger to point at Thibault, as if he wished to curse him, too, before his hand fell to his side, as lifeless as the rest of him.

Romein closed the boy's eyes. He would send for Father Laurence to say Last Rites, but first, he must see to the villain who had slain Mercutio, for this child beater could not be allowed to live.

"Mercutio's soul is but a little way above our heads, waiting for yours to keep him company.

Either you or I must go with him, and I vow it shall be you!" Romein seized the knight's sword from its scabbard, and began to hammer its owner's helm. Within moments, he had it ringing like a bell.

"You brought him here, miller, and his blood is on your hands!" Thibault shouted, trying to dodge the blows, but in such heavy armour, he was too slow.

"Romein!" Julia's scream cut through his heart like a blade, distracting him just enough to give Thibault the advantage.

The knight bulled into him, using his greater weight to knock Romein to the ground, just as he had Mercutio.

Romein waited for a punch from that armoured fist to end his life, just like Mercutio's, but the blow never came, for Julia came flying out of nowhere, crashing into Thibault and knocking him to the ground.

Thirty-Eight

Julia saw Romein on the ground, and she didn't think. She just threw herself at Thibault, desperate to keep him away from Romein. They landed beside a boy, another of Thibault's victims, judging by the pool of blood beneath him.

But Thibault recovered before Julia did, seizing her around the waist and lifting her into the air. "You will learn your place, bitch!" he growled, shaking her until her teeth rattled. "Or maybe you are too much trouble. I had thought to enjoy you for a little while before you met your untimely death…poison slipped into your wine cup, and you would simply go to sleep and not wake…but now, I think it is better to end things now. I shall slip some coins to the priest, who will record our marriage on the day I arrived, so that when your father arrives, there is nothing to stop me from taking Veluwe as my own, as is my right. But first, I shall teach you to be silent." He carried her inexorably toward the rushing sound of the river, then shoved her in, face first.

Julia tried to scream, but all she did was inhale a mouthful of water instead. Water – the only element her magic could touch. She bit her lip, her lungs burning for a breath, and let out the last of her air with a whispered plea for the water to help her.

Coolness touched her face, like a soft breeze stroking her cheeks. Julia gasped, inhaling blessed air, before she convulsed in a fit of coughing, bringing up the water she'd swallowed. She was still under the water, held there by Thibault's heavy hand, but now, she could breathe.

She stopped fighting, willing her body to relax, as she tried to take deep breaths from the air bubble the river had given her. Surely Thibault would give up, and release her.

When he did, water seized her limbs, carrying her out of his grasp, and deeper into the river channel. She floated on the current, drifting in the murky depths, until she glimpsed a flash of silver. A fish, she thought, reaching for it, but it was colder, heavier than any fish.

No, in her hand she held a sword – the same sword Romein had raised to block her path on the day they met. A weapon that had lain on the river bed, waiting for the day Romein would face Thibault again.

But he would not face him alone.

Thirty-Nine

Romein wasn't sure how long he lay there, stunned by the bastard's blow. It might have been a second, or it might have been an hour. But his first waking thought was for Julia – he must protect Julia. He clambered to his feet, casting about for his wife, and for Mercutio's killer. Only to see them on the river bank – the knave on his knees, with her in the water, submerged to the waist, her heels drumming on the shore as he drowned her.

"I am your foe, not her! Fight me instead, coward!" Romein shouted, but the knave did not hear, so intent was he on holding Julia down.

Romein picked up a stone and threw it. It clanged off Thibault's back. He threw more, each ringing louder as he came closer, but still Thibault did not release Julia.

And then…Julia's feet stopped moving, and Romein's heart stopped with them.

Only then did Thibault release her, pushing her out into the water where she sank like a stone.

Romein lost all reason in that moment, for his mind knew only rage.

Not Julia. Not sweet, saintly Julia, who did not deserve to die by violence, least of all at the hands of her own kin.

He pounded on the knight's helmet, beating at his chest. Somehow, he lost the knight's sword, and fought with only his fists. Until an armoured fist landed deep in Romein's gut, punching the breath out of his lungs.

He was dimly aware of hitting the ground, snow cushioning his fall, a mercy it had not given to Mercutio, before the knight seized his feet and began to drag him. First along the frozen ground, then along cold cobblestones, until he realised they were on the bridge.

The knight hoisted him up over his head. Romein was no longer the skinny boy he'd been seven years ago — it took all the knight's considerable strength, and he could hear the man breathing hard inside his helm.

For seven years, Romein had racked his brain, wondering what he could have done differently so that he did not end up in the river with a broken leg and smashed ribs that day. He'd learned to walk, then fight unarmed, and with a sword, and yet here he was, about to fall from the bridge one final time.

Romein surveyed the river. Julia's body should have floated to the surface now, but there was no sign of her. The river that nearly took his life seven years ago would be her grave.

"Either you or I or both shall go with her," Romein muttered.

Mercutio deserved a companion with which to walk the afterlife, but angelic Julia deserved an honour guard to march her into heaven. Romein would share her grave, God willing, for it would be their marriage bed.

If only fate were not so fickle, he would find a way to avoid going into the river. And yet…if that was where Julia was, why should he fight?

All his work with waterwheels and windmills, with Julia, had been to save this river and the lands around it. After Julia's death and his own, who would save it now? Not Thibault, whose very presence polluted the land Julia had loved. For Julia's sake, he could not be allowed to befoul it any longer.

"Your or I or both must go with her…and I choose both!"

Romein could not stop Thibault from tossing him in the river – he never could – but this time, with his knowledge of weight and power, force and how to apply it, he would see Thibault fall, too.

Romein fastened his legs about the knight's neck, then dived for the water, dragging the knave in after him.

Forty

Julia's sodden gown weighed her down, and the sword slowed her even further, but finally, she made it to the river bank, and lay sprawled on the stones.

Romein – where was Romein?

A shout echoed across the water, and for one terrible moment, she saw Thibault lift Romein into the air.

No…not again…She pushed herself to her feet, using Romein's sword as a crutch when her numb limbs threatened to buckle beneath her. Cold…so cold…she could scarcely struggle to take a step, let alone make it to the bridge before Thibault dropped Romein.

Blood streamed down her hand – she must have cut herself without realising it. Shivering, she stepped up to the river's edge, holding her hand out so the blood dripped into the river instead. The river that had saved her, and now she paid the price for the blood magic which allowed the river to understand her words, as she prayed that the waters would protect Romein, too.

The river swirled, her blood eddying around in a dizzying circle, before a wave began to build. The sort of wave one saw on the open ocean, in a storm, but never on their quiet river without a flood to stoke its rage. Her blood fuelled this, she knew, for she could clearly see the red streaks in the foam as the wave rose up and up, higher than the bank, higher than the bridge, higher than the waterwheel…before crashing over the top of the bridge, Thibault, Romein, stone arch and all.

And when the water had washed away…only the bridge was left. Both men were gone.

She stumbled along the river bank, desperately searching for Romein, but there was no sign of him. Weeping, she mounted the bridge, so cold she could scarcely feel the stones under her feet. She would throw herself into the river after him, and together…

A faint cough sounded down by her feet. Julia blinked, hardly daring to believe what she was seeing. Romein lay on the stones, wedged against the side of the bridge, as soaked as she was. He struggled to his feet, and pulled her close.

They stood there for a moment, too thankful to hold one another again to care about anything but each other, until a creaking groan rent the air.

The waterwheel had begun to move. Slowly, at first, before it began to turn steadily, as though Romein's sails still drove it. But there were no sails today – only the river current. This was the river's work.

The water around the wheel began to change colour. At first, it was just faint pink, before it turned to red, a spreading pool that streamed away in the current. And in the middle, a leather eye patch floated up, bearing the fleur-de-lis, before it was swept beneath the bridge downstream.

Forty-One

"We should get out of these clothes, and inside, where it is warm and dry," Romein said.

Julia nodded, leaning on him as they limped toward the mill.

Once inside, Julia headed upstairs to get some blankets, while Romein built up the fire. He stripped off his clothes and hung them in front of the hearth, then accepted a blanket from Julia.

"You know, we could just take these blankets back upstairs, and start our wedding night early. I know of no law that says a man can only make love to his wife after the sun has set," Romein said.

"I do not know much about such things at all. Only that it is a wife's duty…" Julia closed her eyes. Her mother had called it a duty, but her brothers had called it a joy.

Romein took her hand. "Then I shall teach you what I know, and everything else, we can find out together."

She followed him upstairs, then climbed into the box bed after him, closing the doors behind them so that the only light was the flickering candle in a lantern, high up on the wall.

She opened with a kiss, as his lips met hers, until her tongue entered the fray, eagerly wishing to taste if Romein was as sweet as she remembered. Then his hands joined the dance, gliding over her skin beneath the blankets, until she had no further need of scratchy wool, for all she wanted to feel against her body was him.

Her pleasure at his touch started as slow tingles, bubbling beneath her skin like a breath blown out under the water, but it built quickly, turning into a raging torrent until she was overcome by waves so powerful, she was powerless to do anything but cling to him and cry out his name, until she surfaced from an ocean of bliss to take another life-giving breath.

Only to hear his own hoarse voice caress her name, a cry so rough and raw, and yet it was the sweetest sound she had ever heard.

And if they slept for a time, it was only to wake to the bloom of heat between them, as they made love again.

Forty-Two

Spring had melted the last of the winter snows, and the fruit trees in Julia's orchard had begun to bloom before another Capet came to Veluwe. But it was not Father, as Thibault had told her, or a company of his men. No, it was her oldest brother, Aran, and he rode alone.

"This is a strange country you live in," he greeted her, as he kissed her cheeks. "For the last day, I have ridden past a number of structures with sails. Never in my life have I seen sails on land before, and here, they seem to sprout like mushrooms. What sort of madness is here?"

Julia laughed. After the success of Romein's first windmill, they had built them everywhere, to drain the snowmelt away from the fields, first to mine them for salt, and then to plant crops for the next season. "They are mills, like horse mills, only the sails driven by the wind power them. Most of them pump water out of the fields, to stop them from flooding. The plans came from Queen Molina to my husband, and who are we to refuse a royal decree?" She shrugged, and her shawl slipped from her shoulders. It was a wedding gift from Lady Mona, woven swirls of pink and blue wool, and so large she could almost use it for a cloak.

"Ah, yes, your husband. Father had us all ready to set out to Veluwe for your wedding, but he was laid low on the very eve of our journey, and he did not recover." Aran hung his head. "Forgive me for being the bearer of bad tidings, but Father has passed to his eternal rest. His final words were of you, and how he intended to make Veluwe a wedding gift to you and your new husband. He made me promise I would give these lands to you instead. Yet he never did tell me what manner of man you married."

"He is a good man, and a noble one. Honourable, too, with a terrible thirst for knowledge. He is one of the Queen's favourites, and he has her ear. The Queen even sent us a wedding gift…" A book filled with the most lurid pictures of couples…and sometimes more than couples, abed. She dared not show it to her brother, for every picture made her blush so hot her cheeks burned. "He has been a great help, managing the estates at Veluwe, especially repairing the damage from the last floods. Father could not have chosen a better husband for me."

"And are you happy?" Aran asked.

Ah, he was as perceptive as William. If she lied, he would know.

"I have never been happier than I am now, as Romein's wife. For a time, I thought our fates so star-crossed that my life was doomed to tragedy, but Romein, with his windmills and other modern notions, has quite changed my mind. In fact, I would challenge anyone, man or woman, to deny that our life together will be lived any other way than happily ever after."

"Not I, certainly, for I wish you and Romein every happiness. Though I cannot imagine these windmills will remain in use for long."

"Fate will decide, as she always does, to the surprise of some, and the gratitude of others," Julia said.

But fate had already decided that this pair of star-crossed lovers had suffered enough, and their future held only happiness.

As for Thibault, no one ever did find his body, though his horse was found outside a lonely inn, a known gambling den, which the knight had often frequented in the past. The inn patrons merely shrugged, and played a round of dice to see who would claim his horse. And then forgot about Sir Thibault of Paris, tourney champion and Prince of Cats.

Demelza Carlton has always loved the ocean, but on her first snorkelling trip she found she was afraid of fish.

She has since swum with sea lions, sharks and sea cucumbers and stood on spray drenched cliffs over a seething sea as a seven-metre cyclonic swell surged in, shattering a shipwreck below.

Demelza now lives in Perth, Western Australia, the shark attack capital of the world.

The *Ocean's Gift* series was her first foray into fiction, followed by her suspense thriller *Nightmares* trilogy. She swears the *Mel Goes to Hell* series ambushed her on a crowded train and wouldn't leave her alone.

Want to know more? You can follow Demelza on Facebook, Twitter, YouTube or her website, Demelza Carlton's Place at:

www.demelzacarlton.com

More Books by Demelza Carlton

<u>Colony: Holiday series</u>

Cowboys and Aliens (#1)

Ghost (#2)

Vulcan (#3)

Cupid (#4)

Valentine(#5)

Prometheus (#6)

<u>**Colony: Aqua series**</u>

Halcyon (#1)

Poseidon (#2)

Apollo (#3)

<u>**Colony: Nyx series**</u>

Fang (#1)

Talon (#2)

Claw (#3)

<u>**Siren of Secrets series**</u>

Ocean's Secret (#1)

Ocean's Gift (#2)

Ocean's Infiltrator (#3)

<u>**Nightmares Trilogy**</u>

Nightmares of Caitlin Lockyer (#1)

Necessary Evil of Nathan Miller (#2)

Afterlife of Alana Miller (#3)

<u>**Romance Island Resort series**</u>

Maid for the Rock Star (#1)

The Rock Star's Email Order Bride (#2)

The Rock Star's Virginity (#3)

The Rock Star and the Billionaire (#4)

The Rock Star Wants A Wife (#5)

The Rock Star's Wedding (#6)

Maid for the South Pole (#7)

<u>**Romance a Medieval Fairytale series**</u>

Enchant: Beauty and the Beast Retold

Dance: Cinderella Retold

Fly: Goose Girl Retold

Revel: Twelve Dancing Princesses Retold

Silence: Little Mermaid Retold

Awaken: Sleeping Beauty Retold

Embellish: Brave Little Tailor Retold

Appease: Princess and the Pea Retold

Blow: Three Little Pigs Retold

Return: Hansel and Gretel Retold

Wish: Aladdin Retold

Melt: Snow Queen Retold

Spin: Rumpelstiltskin Retold

Kiss: Frog Prince Retold

Reflect: Snow White Retold

Roar: Goldilocks Retold

Cobble: Elves and the Shoemaker Retold

Float: Enchanted Horse Retold

Steal: Forty Thieves Retold

Call: Pied Piper Retold

Fall: Scheherazade Retold

Feather: Swan Maidens Retold

Cross: Billy Goats Gruff Retold

Weave: Rapunzel Retold

Claim: Puss in Boots Retold

Curse: Rose Red Retold

Cross: Three Billy Goats Gruff Retold

Weave: Rapunzel Retold

Claim: Puss in Boots Retold

<u>**Heart of Stone series**</u>

Heart of Steel (#0)

Broken Chains (#1)

Broken Bonds (#2)

Broken Dreams (#3)

<u>**Heart of Steel series**</u>

Heart of Steel (#0)

Stone Guardian (#1)

Stone Champion (#2)

Stone Sentinel (#3)

Stone Shadow (#4)